The Best of Families

ALSO BY HARRY GROOME

Wing Walking
Thirty Below
The Girl Who Fished with a Worm

The Best of Families

a novel

Harry Groome

THE
CONNELLY
PRESS

for my sister Peggy and my brother Clark

By love, the bitter becomes sweet…
By love, pain becomes healing.
—*Rumi*

There comes a time when you realize that everything is a dream, and only those things preserved in writing have any possibility of being real.
—*James Salter*

My Family; Our Story

Mark Twain once wrote, "In Boston they ask, how much does he know? In New York, how much is he worth? In Philadelphia, who were his parents?"

As a Philadelphian I'll answer that provocative question this way: My name is Francis Hopkinson Delafield Jr.—Fran to most everyone—and I was born into one of the city's oldest families, a family of *Social Register*-registered blue bloods who were born on third base but thought we'd gotten there by hitting a triple. Without a doubt, we Delafields are a nest of good old-fashioned WASPs: unimaginative, out-of-touch, sporting Bermuda shorts, bow ties, and Capezios...well, the list goes on and on, but I think old Mr. Twain would get the picture. And, although it goes well beyond what he asked, of course we're all products of private school educations. Every entitled one of us.

What's more, having learned how my connection with my parents—I don't know the proper term for it: biological, cultural, spiritual, genetic?—has shaped my life, I understand why my sister, Heather, always says that everything that takes place in our parents' circle of friends is tribal. And over time I've gotten a better grip on why it's easier for them to stay rooted in the past than to face the changes the future might bring, certainly the kind of changes that I've forced my parents to accept.

Heather also was the person who thought it would be a good idea for me to confront my past rather than sweep it under the rug the way I do most things. Write it all down, is what she said— hence this midlife memoir, or whatever you might choose to call it. She thought it might help me understand, maybe even help me forgive, a lot of what's happened in our family, and from this I guess you can tell that, as uncomfortable as parts of this will be for me to tell, Heather thought it might heal some old family wounds, maybe even help me learn some things I needed to know.

So to begin, a little bit of background.

In 1941, just before my father went off to the war, we moved to 1212 Poor Richard's Lane in Chestnut Hill, to a cinderblock-and-glass house that Dad had designed and which Mom and he have ever since referred to as "Twelve-Twelve," as if it were a Newport mansion or a building of similar historical significance. With the 23 trolley clanking up and down its cobblestone main street, Chestnut Hill, both fashionable and unhurried in its pace, could easily have been a Hollywood set, even a Norman Rockwell *Saturday Evening Post* cover. It was there that Mom saw our family as members of the "impoverished aristocracy" and viewed herself as one of Philadelphia's grandes dames. And, after the war, it was where she and Dad entertained their well-heeled friends, rolling back the worn rug in the living room and drinking and smoking and dancing into the wee hours of the morning to the big bands— Benny Goodman, Glenn Miller, Artie Shaw—as though they never again would have a care in the world.

But Twelve-Twelve is more than just a place where my parents entertained. It's where Heather and I grew into our teens, doing pretty much everything that was expected of us. Maybe even a little more. Heather was a high-honor student, president of her class, and captain of the field hockey team at the nearby girls' school.

I started at the local day school for boys but, after eighth grade, went away to the Episcopal School in New Hampshire, just like my grandfather, father, and Mom's brother, my uncle Robert Peltier, had before me.

I think that's enough history and will begin my story in 1955. I was eighteen, had just graduated from Episcopal, and was on my way to a summer job in Quebec with my closest friend, Potter Morris. As you will see, this trip, as brief as it was, set the cornerstone for all that follows and altered my life forever. Please know that many of the revelations that I uncover here—several of which my family have jealously kept secret from the outside world—may come as a surprise to you because a number of them aren't exactly what you'd expect of a family like mine.

Francis H. Delafield, Jr.
September 1968

1955

La Malbaie

A popular travel guide described La Malbaie as "a picturesque village ninety miles northeast of Quebec City where the Malbaie River empties into the north shore of the St. Lawrence. One of Canada's original vacation resorts, La Malbaie is home to a patchwork of small dairy farms, a number of elegant inns, and a large paper mill."

That large mill was owned by Malbaie Papier, the town's major employer, and was where Potter and I had planned to work until we went off to college. Our awkward working arrangement was the result of a deal struck between Potter's father, then a top executive at Scott Paper, and a wealthy colleague and one of Scott Paper's major suppliers, a man named J. P. Trudeau. Potter's father had not only enlisted Monsieur Trudeau to hire Potter but to board him as well, and when Potter was given permission to bring a friend, he invited me to join him. I knew the opportunity would make my mother happy because it would give me a chance to use my French even though, as Mom put it, "those Quebecois mangle the language so badly." And when the plan finally fell into place, it pleased both our fathers as well, something that was of the utmost importance to Potter and me, for when our fathers began to trickle back from the war and tried to pry the family circle open to make room for themselves again, they had become our bigger-than-life heroes.

Not only had they kept us safe from the Nazis and the Japs (people I couldn't even imagine but had seen on the RKO-Pathé newsreels at the movies and feared and hated nonetheless), they reappeared in our homes in sharply creased uniforms with colorful patches on their sleeves and shiny indicators on their thick shoulders of how important they were, and we stood in awe of them.

How could boys of eight, as Potter and I were when the war ended, not want to please these men, to measure up for them? Especially if they had prescribed standards of performance for us, whether they be grades in school, decorum on the athletic field, or courage on the street.

And, while in many ways Potter was no different from me and many of our friends, I always thought he tried harder than most to please his father by following in his footsteps every step of the way. Like his father he, too, went to the Episcopal School and was on his way to Princeton where he would become a member of the Ivy Club—the same eating club Mr. Morris had joined—and after graduation would get his MBA from the Wharton School and go to work for a white-shoe Philadelphia company, again just like his dad.

While I thought it was understandable (even excusable) because Potter's father lectured him on what to do at every turn, it made me wonder why Dad did just the opposite, always encouraging me to work things out for myself. I must admit that in many ways I appreciated the feeling of independence and maturity that Dad's approach instilled in me, but at times it made me wonder if he genuinely cared for me; if he could be bothered to attend to me; or, worse, if he would be there for me when I really needed him.

<hr />

Late June, Potter and I were chauffeured from the train station in Quebec City to La Malbaie by René Jaud, an employee of M. Trudeau's. No more than five feet five inches tall, René had pale, waxy skin and a sloppy paunch and gripped the steering wheel of his boss's Mercedes convertible with hands that would have better fit a man twice his size. At first I thought that the baby-blue beret that he wore was the way Potter and I were to identify him, but soon learned that the beret was pure René, as was Babette, the nervous miniature poodle with the pink bows tied at the base of her white ears that curled in his lap as he drove.

During the ride to La Malbaie, I slumped in the backseat, saying little while listening to Potter and René chatter, although every once in a while I'd place a hand on the back of Potter's seat and pull myself forward to join in the conversation. On the first such occasion, René had asked Potter what he and his friend liked to do.

Potter took his time answering while he lit a Lucky Strike. "You know. The usual."

It was clear from Potter's response that he wasn't enjoying René's questions, a fact that apparently wasn't lost on René either, because he began to smile and then contained it. "And the usual is? Golf? Fishing? Tennis?" He paused and ran a hand over the crown of Babette's curly white head. "Girls?"

Potter said yes, he played a lot of tennis and squash and had been the junior tennis champion at the Philadelphia Cricket Club. He added that when there wasn't a scheduling conflict with the baseball team at Episcopal, he played wherever the school needed him on the tennis team.

"Fantastic," René said. "I think you will enjoy your tennis with Monsieur Trudeau. He is a very good player as well."

Potter nodded and winked at me and then looked back to René. "And, yes, I have a girlfriend. Her name is Sidney." When he cupped his hands in front of his chest, I knew all too well what was coming, for I'd heard it many, many times before. I tapped him on the shoulder and gave him a you've-got-to-be-kidding, are-you-out-of-your-mind? look, but Potter simply chuckled. "Sidney with the bodacious hogans. They're like Lucky Strikes, René. So round, so firm, so fully packed."

René made a *pfiff* sound. "And your friend?"

"Fran," Potter reminded him.

"Of course," René said. "Monsieur Francis Hopkinson Delafield whose ancestor signed your Declaration of Independence—"

"And designed the American flag," Potter interrupted.

"*Ah, oui?*" René said.

"*Ah, oui,*" Potter answered, using up at least a quarter of his conversational French.

René chuckled, shook his head, and a made his *pfiff* sound again. "And who can throw a baseball very fast. No?"

Potter smiled and pounded his fist into his open left hand. "Fran the man's got a hummer, that's for sure."

When I said that I hoped to pitch in college, that I didn't have a girlfriend and didn't play golf or tennis, René shook his head and muttered, "*Tant pis.*"

I slumped back into my seat and thought, "Too bad is right, but nothing new," for while Potter and I lived in Chestnut Hill and went to the same schools, and our parents had many friends in common, little did anyone outside our family understand that that's where our similarities ended. All Heather's and my friends had summer homes in the Poconos or along the coast of Rhode Island or, like Potter, on Mount Desert Island in Maine, often referred to by the in-group as "Philadelphia on the Rocks." All, that is, except for my family, and one of the things that sticks in my mind about my childhood is how uncomfortable the summers were, not only because of the heat and the humidity but because of the boredom.

My summers—until I was old enough to drive and get a job—were filled with swimming endless laps in our small pool with Al Jolson, our Labrador retriever, and playing catch with myself by throwing a tennis ball against our cinder-block chimney for hours on end. As a result, golf, tennis, and squash were some of the key—and embarrassing—indicators of our differences. While all of my friends' parents belonged to private clubs where my peers were taught to play these sports from an early age, their lessons including the correct grip and stroke or swing, and the rules and the etiquette and dress, my family didn't belong to any clubs, with the exception of my father's lapsed membership in the Philadelphia Club, his resignation signaling a turning point in my awareness of exactly where our family stood in the financial pecking order.

The phone had rung during the sacred cocktail hour: six thirty to seven thirty every night, come rain or come shine. Mom answered the phone and looked to Dad. "Theo, it's Henry," she said. Rather than taking the phone that she reached toward him, Dad stood and walked to the far side of the small phone table, set his old-fashioned on it, smoothed his tie and buttoned his perfectly fitting Brooks Brothers suit jacket, and lifted the phone gently from Mom's outstretched hand.

The caller was Henry Pearson, my godfather and the president of the Philadelphia Club. The conversation was short but collegial. After greetings and a protracted silence, my father said, "It's kind of you to ask and for the club to offer, but I'm afraid I can't accept, Henry. We've got one too many scholarship students here right now without me being added to the list. Maybe someday I'll be able to rejoin, but for now you'll have to accept my resignation in the spirit in which it's offered."

When Dad hung up, he placed his hand on Mom's shoulder as she tried to fight back tears. "It was the right thing to do, Gay," he said. "With the second mortgage, we'll be through the worst of this in no time."

"But, Theo, what will people say?" she asked. "It's such a comedown, so humiliating, and everyone will know. *Sacrebleu.* It puts us even further on the fringe." She took a last swallow of her old-fashioned, swirled the remaining ice in circles, and raised her glass. "*Un soupcon, s'il vous plait.*"

Although I was only thirteen at the time, I realized that discussions about scholarships weren't about my grades or Heather's but were about money. I've never forgotten that phone call because that evening our parents made it clear that, wherever Heather was to go to college, she had to be offered a scholarship, and if I was to go to Episcopal, the school would have to provide financial aid. Further, as Heather and I silently ate dinner and listened to our parents' musings, it became apparent that there was an unspoken agreement within our family that our embarrassing financial circumstances were to be a tightly held secret. Perhaps so no one would gossip about us, or worse, take pity on us.

As these uncomfortable thoughts ran through my mind, René asked Potter if he spoke French, a question that drew me forward from the backseat once again.

"*Au contraire,*" Potter said with a laugh and added quickly, "but Delafield does."

"But you do not?" René said.

Potter shook his head.

"It may be a difficult summer for you."

"We'll see," Potter said. "My old man promised me that Mr. Trudeau would find a way to make it work."

"Interesting," René said in French. "And, Fran, you are fluent, no?"

I said yes, that my mother spoke French and that my sister and I had learned from her, as well as at school.

René laughed. "Perhaps you should have brought your mother to help Potter."

"I'm Potter's guest, not the other way around," I said, wondering if this was just a failed attempt at humor on Rene's part or if he was going to be a pain in the ass all summer, and we rode in silence for the last half hour to La Malbaie.

Monsieur Trudeau

When we arrived, René introduced Monsieur Trudeau's summer residence that overlooked the village and the St. Lawrence River with theatrical sweeps of his large hands, describing it as "*la incomparable maison*." After conducting a tour of the house, René showed us to our cabins, telling us that dinner would be served at seven *précis*, at which time we would meet our host. As he turned to leave, he gave Potter a curious look and asked if he understood *précis*. Before Potter could answer, I assured him that he—that we—understood.

After René left, Potter lit a cigarette and gave him the finger. "See if you understand the old *oiseau*, you little douchebag," he said, and told me that it was going to be a long summer if he had to put up with too much more shit from René about his not speaking French.

A comparison of our cabins showed them to be almost identical. Each had a cramped bedroom with a single bed highlighted by a colorfully striped Hudson Bay blanket. Each also had a sitting area that contained a small couch, an easy chair, and a low, knotty-pine coffee table stacked with dog-eared copies of *Field & Stream* and *Outdoor Life*. A black bear's head snarled above the wood stove in my cabin, while a moose head hung forlornly above the stove in Potter's.

I was unpacking when Potter tapped on my door and said he'd be back in a moment, that he was going to hunt down René and find out how to call home. I waited until close to seven for him to return and then hurried to the dining room where I hoped that I'd find him. Instead, I was greeted by a tall man with perfect posture and impeccably groomed white hair who wore a purple velvet dinner jacket and a white shirt with a paisley ascot billowing from its open collar. Behind him, René paced the length of the long dining table with Babette cradled in his arms.

The man removed his gold-rimmed Ben Franklin glasses, folded them with small, precise movements, and smiled. "My dear Potter, it's so nice to finally meet you. I am so fond of your father."

I quickly introduced myself as Potter's friend, trying to correct him as diplomatically as I could, and said that Potter would be along shortly, that he was trying to call home. M. Trudeau apologized for the confusion and extended his right hand, which was missing its index finger. I reached somewhat tentatively to shake it as René tapped his watch. "Fran, where is he?" he asked in French. "It is well past seven, and Monsieur Trudeau does not like to be kept waiting. Didn't I emphasize that 'precisely' means just that, precisely?"

I apologized again for Potter and repeated that he was trying to call home, that I was sure he'd be there any minute.

M. Trudeau waved a hand as though he was fanning himself and looked to René. "No matter. Please have my dinner delivered to the library in twenty minutes. Perhaps I will meet the phantom Potter Morris tomorrow evening." He smiled at me, clicked his patent leather dinner pumps together, and gave a short bow to excuse himself. "Your mother has taught you well. You shouldn't have any problem at the mill."

My first thought was, if René had told M. Trudeau about my mother teaching me French, had he also told him about Potter's limited language skills? I wondered how they planned to overcome that obstacle. While I was trying to work this through, I registered that there were only three place settings at the long table, signaling that M. Trudeau wasn't going to eat with Potter and me. I turned to the man whom I now realized was to babysit my friend and me for the summer and, from the look on his face, I sensed that René was no happier with the situation than I was.

"I thought for sure he'd be here by now," I said.

René threw a hand in the air in disgust and made his *pfiff* sound. He reached for a small silver bell on the dining table and shook it angrily, announcing that it was time to eat, with or without my unreliable friend, and then asked, "What could possibly be keeping him?"

I shrugged and wondered, what indeed? What phone call could be that important? Checking in with his father? With Sidney? And how the hell could he abandon me on our first night in this foreign place?

A few minutes later, Potter joined us, explaining that he'd encountered problems getting through to the States. René simply raised his eyebrows, and we finished our meal in silence, each occasionally looking up from our food and forcing a smile.

After the dessert plates had been cleared, René outlined what our first day at the mill would entail and said in French that breakfast would be served punctually at seven. He turned to Potter. "Do you understand?"

Potter shrugged and looked to me.

"We understand," I said and shot a stern look at Potter. "And we will be on time."

"*Mon Dieu,*" René mumbled as he wished us good night. "This is going to be a very interesting experiment."

Un Grand Saumon

As you will soon learn, we didn't work in the mill for very long, and my memories of the little work I did come to me in flashes, the images nothing more than a muted black and white. The things I do remember are the deafening noise of the rollers, the pervasive, sweet smell of the pulp, and the small gray room where I spent each day checking pressure gauges—gauges I'm convinced were electronically monitored, my employment being nothing more than a favor to Potter's father from M. Trudeau.

My memories of what happened outside the mill, however, are as clear as if they took place yesterday.

To start, the cold war between Potter and René thawed a bit, although not completely, and in time René abandoned his frequent criticisms of Potter's inability to speak French, especially after Potter showed us the sign language that he and his supervisor had developed to communicate. It was a cross between charades—two words, sounds like, looks like—and hand and finger signals for things like "check the gauges at ten o'clock." Potter delivered all in a comedic pantomime that so amused René that he insisted Potter put on the same performance for M. Trudeau, thinking, I would guess, that it would help put M. Trudeau's mind at ease about the awkward position he found himself in.

Of even more importance, near the end of our first week, René asked Potter and me if we'd like to go fishing. "It is your Independence Day weekend, and there will be other Americans in the camp."

I quickly volunteered that, although I'd never been fishing before, it sounded like fun to me, and I was convinced that Potter would say the same, mainly because I had no idea of what we were to do on weekends. Much to my surprise, however, Potter declined, saying that he'd promised M. Trudeau that he'd be his tennis partner over the weekend.

Not unlike whom he talked with during his nightly phone calls, Potter's tennis plans also had been a well-kept secret, and the familiar feeling of being on the outside looking in rather than being a member of the inner circle washed over me. While I sensed that I'd be nothing more than a fifth wheel if I stayed with Potter while he and M. Trudeau played tennis, I was uneasy about leaving the security of my friend's company. I thought this type of thing happened to me more often than I would like, and I was frustrated that I still hadn't learned how to cope with these situations and the feelings that accompanied them.

René sensed my discomfort and asked if I still wanted to go. "The river is at a good height," he said, "and the fishing could be excellent. But it is up to you. I will be going no matter what."

"I'm in," I said and glared at Potter. "There's nothing for me to do here."

The trip to the Gaspé began with René speeding—as always with Babette in his lap—along the north shore of the St. Lawrence to catch the ferry from St. Siméon to Rivière-du-Loup. From there we continued along the northern perimeter of the Gaspé Peninsula until close to midnight when, after jostling over a rock-studded dirt road that I was sure would tear apart the undercarriage of M. Trudeau's low-slung Mercedes, René eased the car down a sharp incline and stopped in front of a small cabin. "Welcome to the St. Jean Salmon Club," he said and switched off the headlights.

When my eyes adjusted to the dark, it became clear that we were on the edge of a small compound of cabins that seemed to be hiding from us in the foreboding black. Suddenly I felt uneasy and very, very out of place. Perhaps it was my unfamiliarity with wild places, or with fishing and fishing clubs, or not knowing a soul on this adventure except my eccentric French Canadian companion, and I wished that Potter had joined us or that I'd stayed with him, as sparse as our friendship had become since we'd arrived in La Malbaie.

Before I said a word, René rolled down his window. "Listen, Fran. That beautiful music is the St. Jean River. She's where we will catch the big ones tomorrow."

I knew he expected me to say something enthusiastic, but I couldn't muster anything and lowered my window and listened to the rush of the river and the wind in the trees. A chill came over me, and I confessed for what seemed like the hundredth time, "Don't forget, René, I've never fished before, and my casting will be even worse than Potter's French."

René let out a louder than usual *pfiff* and laughed. "That is hard to believe," he said and promised that he'd teach me all I needed to know as he opened the car door and lowered Babette to the grass.

I woke early with sunlight streaming through the window of my log-walled room. The light and my continued unease with the situation kept me from slipping back to sleep and, after tossing and turning for another hour, I readied myself to start my day. As I stepped from the shower, René shuffled into the bathroom wearing a pair of pale blue skivvies that dug into his doughy upper thighs and drooping belly, and his eyes brightened when he saw me.

It was the first time I'd ever been aware of a man blatantly studying my body, and I quickly wrapped my towel around my waist. René laughed at my modesty and said, "Do not be ashamed. You are very athletically built. An Adonis."

I scoffed at the comment and said that I trained hard for the sports I played, nervously adding that it was something my father had put a lot of emphasis on since I first picked up a ball and a glove. René nodded, seemingly in appreciation. Not knowing what else to do or say, I brushed by him, mumbled something about getting dressed for breakfast, and closed myself in my room.

A few moments later, René knocked lightly on my door. He held Babette in one arm and a pair of chest waders in his free hand. He said the waders were for me, then he hung them on the wood peg outside my door and said we should make our way to breakfast. As we approached the dining cabin, I could hear men talking and laughing in the kitchen, their voices coming in waves, rolling over one another, their comments frequently punctuated with a laugh. Their deep, confident tones caused me to pause on the stairs, again wondering if I belonged in this place, knowing that I was definitely out of my element, once more wishing that I'd stayed with Potter.

The men at the breakfast table stopped talking when René and I entered the room, and before I could focus on the strangers' faces, out of the corner of my eye, I saw a tall man stand and heard a familiar voice. "Why, Fran Delafield, what in the hell are you doing here?"

The man was Bill Ames, a great friend of my parents and the local ear, nose, and throat specialist who had attended to me many times when I was a kid. Still clutching his napkin, Dr. Ames hurried around the table and greeted me while René was already busy joking with the other fishermen, all members of the St. Jean Salmon Club—all friends of M. Trudeau.

After introducing me to everyone, Dr. Ames insisted that I sit next to him, requiring one of the men to move his place setting, and although he did it with good humor and understanding, I—being the youngest in the group by at least twenty-five years, not knowing a soul, and never having fished a day in my life—was embarrassed by the commotion I'd created, the commotion that had made me the center of attention.

As we ate, Dr. Ames also insisted that he give me a casting lesson and that the fishing pairings be rearranged so he and I could fish together. At first René argued that I was his responsibility, but, in the end, Dr. Ames's quiet but steel-willed bedside manner and the unspoken fact that he was a member of the club, and not a member's hired hand, prevailed.

Later, I was relieved that it was Dr. Ames who was teaching me to cast and not René, because when he stood behind me and held my hand that worked the rod, his touch was comforting, his smell familiar, much like Dad's—the smell of shaving soap mixed with cigarettes and something else, something I always associated with being a man. And for a moment I was a child again, once again in the care of the man who had helped me through so many painful moments.

(When I was nine or ten, I got lots of abscessed ears, creating a real dilemma because with each abscess, I had to wrestle with how long I would endure the pain before I told my parents and succumbed to the unpleasant routine that was bound to follow. Dr. Ames would tiptoe into my bedroom and set his black physician's bag at the foot of the bed and then look down at me with large brown eyes made even larger by his thick glasses. He would smile and pat my leg and ask which ear it was this time while he slipped on a worn leather headband that held a round mirror with a hole in its middle. After he'd examined the ear, he'd ask if I was ready and then say, "Okay, champ, here we go again," and shake ether onto a gauze patch and press it gently over my nose and mouth. I have to admit that I never figured out which was worse, the pain of the earache or the smell of ether, but that smell has haunted me ever since. When I woke up, Dr. Ames would be taking my blood pressure and my pulse. He'd ask if I was feeling better and smile and say, "That's a wrap on earaches, okay?" and leave as quickly as he'd arrived.)

But now Dr. Ames was urging me to imagine that I was holding a book between the elbow of my casting arm and my side, all the while letting me feel the rhythm that a decent cast required while quietly chanting, "Stop at one o'clock on the back cast and nine o'clock going forward."

My first attempt to catch an Atlantic salmon began with our guide, a gentle giant by the name of Clarence Colford, driving Dr. Ames and me along a dusty road to a series of pools on the St. Jean River, the crystal-clear water tinted the color of crème de menthe, the liqueur that as kids Heather and I had licked from the bottom of the glasses strewn about the living room the mornings following one of our parents' many dinner parties. After Clarence pulled off to the side of the road and the three of us had climbed into our waders, I watched carefully as Clarence and Dr. Ames pointed the split-cane sections of their rods skyward, squinting along them to make sure they were perfectly aligned before forcing them snugly together. Once their reels were firmly in place and their fly lines fed through their rods' guides, Dr. Ames and Clarence questioned each other about what fly they should choose. Clarence selected a Blue Charm for me. Dr. Ames unzipped one of the many pockets on his fishing vest and opened an aluminum box filled with rows of flies. He ran his hand over several, in the end choosing a black fly with a spot of Day-Glo green wool on its butt and holding it up to Clarence for his approval.

Despite all the preparation and the many discussions about fly selection and what must have been at least a thousand clumsy casts, that evening Dr. Ames was forced to make an entry in the club's heavy, leather-bound log that neither he nor I had caught a fish. The fact that four of the other fishermen hadn't caught a fish made it a less bitter pill to swallow until René scolded me, saying that I should have fished with him as M. Trudeau had instructed and, more than once, pointed out that he and his fishing partner had caught three salmon while Dr. Ames and I had caught none.

The next day's schedule put Dr. Ames and me on a stretch of the neighboring York River where we began fishing in the same fashion we had the day before: Dr. Ames would fish through the pool first; then I would wade where he had waded and try to cast where he had cast. Dr. Ames assured me that it didn't make any difference who went first. "If there are taking fish in the river, we'll both catch them" was his promise, and, while I tried hard to accept his logic, the concept didn't make sense to me.

When Dr. Ames waded into the fast-moving water at the head of the York's famous Whitehouse Pool, I asked Clarence if all that the doctor had told me was true.

Clarence smiled. "Salmon fishing is frustrating, no?"

I pressed him in French for a more direct response.

Clarence smiled again and patted me on the shoulder. "The fish will have to answer for themselves. The doctor wants you to catch a fish very badly. I am sure of that. He is a good sport, a good man, so step in the river, do as he does, and see what the fish gods have in store for you." He stripped a few dozen feet of line from my rod and handed it to me. "Here short casts will work well."

And so I began to wade at the same depth as Dr. Ames and tried to imitate all that he did. When he lifted his rod and called to Clarence that he'd just moved a good fish, again I wondered how I could ever catch a fish after this skilled fisherman had the first pass at them, and then the water around my fly bulged and my line straightened and I felt a heavy pull. Before I could say I thought I'd hooked something, Dr. Ames was looking back at me, yelling, "Lift your rod tip and wait for Clarence." Suddenly the fish began to escape down river, and I watched the green fly line disappear from my reel and the reserve of thin yellow backing line grow smaller and smaller and thought that the fish was going to get away, and my heart began to race. I had no idea what to do, when I sensed Clarence close by my shoulder. "I guess the fish gods have answered you." He laughed. "Be patient and do as I say."

The salmon stopped at the tail of the pool at least seventy-five yards from where he'd taken the fly. "He's getting ready to jump," Clarence said. "When he does, bow your rod to him." No sooner had Clarence spoken than the fish curled out of the water, a silver acrobat throwing spray that sparkled in the early morning sun.

Dr. Ames yelled, "Hot damn!" as he backed out of the river.

Clarence whistled and muttered, "My God, but he's a good one," and told me to start reeling and sloshed toward shore, gesturing to me to follow.

To be honest, the next forty-five minutes remain a blur. My nervous system was overloaded with adrenaline, and while the fish continued to run and jump and then stop and sulk and then run and jump again, I tried to follow each piece of advice from Dr. Ames and Clarence, determined beyond all reason to land this fish, perhaps to prove to René—and perhaps to myself as well—that Dr. Ames really was my friend.

Finally, my left arm aching from putting pressure on the fish, my right hand cramped from the endless reeling and re-reeling, the salmon swam just beneath the surface of the water and rolled on its side. Clarence stepped into a slow-moving eddy and rested the basket of his net on the bottom of the river and told me to walk backward and lead the fish over the net. After a number of attempts at what had sounded like such a simple request, barely able to draw a breath, I drew the fish close to Clarence, and he lifted the net, the net suddenly bulging with the curled, heavy salmon. He shook his head in wonderment and said, "*Un grand saumon. Vraiment, un grand saumon.*"

"It sure as hell is," Dr. Ames said. "That's the biggest fish I've ever seen on this river." He reached for my hand. "Well done, son. Very, very well done. She's a beautiful hen, loaded with roe."

"Roe?" I asked.

"Eggs," Dr. Ames said. "She's headed upriver to spawn."

I stared at the enormous fish, thick and powerful but now oddly subdued. I'd never seen anything quite like it before and was smiling broadly when Clarence grasped the salmon by the wrist of her tail, lifted her free from the net, and carried her up on shore where he hit her with a softball-sized rock at the base of her skull several times to kill her.

I stepped from the water and started to ask why he'd done that—after all, she was *my* fish—but thought better of it and told myself to accept this as a customary practice. Still, it felt wrong. Why, I don't know, but I was stung by an urgent sense of loss. I'd never killed anything before and stared at the fish now stretched flat and lifeless on the gravel bank and thought I'd never let this happen again.

Clarence rinsed his hands in the river and reached for mine, offering his congratulations. "They don't get much bigger than this."

"Forty pounds?" Dr. Ames asked.

Clarence guessed thirty-six. His scale hovered between thirty-six and thirty-seven. "We'll call it thirty-seven," Dr. Ames said and looked at me and smiled. "It's okay, Fran. Fishermen are born honest, but we get over it pretty quickly. No matter what, that's one hell of a fish."

A novice catching a thirty-seven-pound salmon caused quite a stir at the club, pleasing me in some ways, but my sense of pride was mixed with misgivings for having ended a living thing's life. In turn I was comforted by the smile that never left Dr. Ames's face, making it clear that everything he'd said and done had been with me in mind.

Little did I know at the time that what happened next would have a far more profound effect on my life than learning to cast a fly or catching a big fish.

Surprise

Our three salmon had been packed with dry ice and sawdust in a crude wood box that was laid carefully in the trunk of the Mercedes, and René was as giddy as a schoolgirl as we began the long drive back to La Malbaie. He referred to me more than once as his pride and joy and boasted in French, "Wait until Monsieur Trudeau learns of this. He will be elated!" Then, after an awkward silence, he said that my catching a giant salmon excited him.

I agreed and said that I'd never experienced anything quite like it.

Unexpectedly, René switched to English. "Do you understand the meanings of the word 'excited'?"

I chuckled and said of course I did. It was the type of question that would have earned him the finger from Potter.

"I don't think so," René said, and took his hand from Babette and placed it on my thigh, slid it toward my groin, and cupped it over me. For an instant I sat frozen in place, then I grabbed René's hand and pushed it to the steering wheel and held it there. A surge of adrenaline, similar to the one that I'd experienced when I'd hooked the salmon, coursed through me, putting me on the offensive. I wanted to punch the son of a bitch silly and told him to keep his hands to himself, that he was a pervert. "A fat, old, fucking pervert."

René turned and briefly looked at me. His tone was soft but firm. "Not a pervert, Fran, a homosexual. There's a difference. A big difference." He waited for me to say something. When I didn't, he added, "I hope you will forgive me. You are a fine young man, and I would like to be your friend."

Bullshit, I thought. Absolute bullshit. He *was* a fucking pervert—a homo, a faggot—and I sat without speaking while I waited for my shaking to subside.

"Well?" René said. "Am I forgiven? Can we be friends?"

Again I didn't answer, and René's tone, while still subdued, took on an air of scolding. "And don't think of reporting this to Monsieur Trudeau. Shall I say, he understands?"

I looked at him, astonished. My host for the summer was a faggot too?

René took a hand from the steering wheel and stroked Babette's head. "All I can say, Fran, is that I'm sorry. Very sorry. This will not happen again, and I really would like to be your friend. If you say no, it will be a very uncomfortable and long summer for both of us."

Without taking my eyes from the road I grunted, "Okay. We're friends. I guess."

"Was that so difficult?" René asked.

It may have been my body's way of releasing the tension from all that had happened that day, but for some reason I began to laugh uncontrollably. "I don't know if it was all that difficult," I said once I'd finally stopped laughing, "but it sure as hell is a new one on me. I've never had a...a...a queer for a friend before."

René laughed, too, and made his familiar *pfiff* sound in kind of a celebratory fashion. "Two new things happened to you today, Fran. Both may last you a long, long time. The first is catching a great salmon. The second is becoming my friend." He offered me his hand, and I shook it and felt a strength in his grip that I hadn't noticed before. "Good," René said. "Now perhaps I can offer you something as a symbol of my friendship. I would like you to meet my niece. She is exactly your age and, if I may say so, is quite wonderful and quite beautiful."

I remember giving him a noncommittal "sounds good to me," wondering if this was more of his bullshit, and slept for most of the rest of the trip home. The few times I woke, I snuck a look at René; each time he seemed to be smiling, and each time I would wonder what his motives were for introducing me to his niece, but I would fall back asleep before I could piece my thoughts together.

———

The dining room was empty when I arrived the next evening, the table set for four rather than the usual three. I thought perhaps M. Trudeau would be joining us for dinner, and I paced nervously, hoping that Potter would curtail his evening phone call and be on time for a change. To my relief, he arrived as the grandfather clock that stood in the corner struck seven. I was about to ask how things were at home, when he put a finger to his lips and nodded toward the doorway where René held Babette, while a girl stood behind him as though she was hiding from Potter and me, her hands folded in front of her, her head bowed, her long black hair falling in front of her face. When she looked up and smiled—uncertainly, I thought—she shied her eyes away from us, and I thought René was right: she was beautiful—far more beautiful than I could have imagined. I also found it hard to believe that she was my age. She was as petite as her uncle, and her face was so young, so innocent, that she looked to be in her early teens. If it hadn't been for the way her breasts pushed against her sleeveless blouse, I would have sworn that her uncle was up to no good again.

René must have sensed what I was thinking and hurriedly introduced Potter and me in English, saying, "This is my niece, Lisette Jaud. She has just graduated from high school and will begin work as the town telephone operator in two weeks when she turns eighteen."

The girl nodded as though she understood what René had said, although I was pretty sure she didn't understand a word. "It is nice to meet you both," she said and smiled at me. "My uncle has told me about your great fish."

Potter gave her a quizzical look and said one of the few things— the very few things—he'd learned since we'd arrived in La Malbaie other than *buvez Coca-Cola glacé.*

"*Parlez-vous Anglais?*" he asked.

"*Un peu,*" Lisette answered, "but not very good."

Potter shrugged, and René suggested that we sit for dinner. Throughout the meal the conversation was halting, but it turned awkward when Potter asked Lisette how she got such a nice tan way up here in the north woods.

René turned to her and said that Potter wanted to know why her skin was the color of café au lait.

For a moment Lisette appeared to be at a loss for words, then she rubbed her forearm with a delicate hand and said that her grandfather was African.

René translated, saying that his niece had a mixed ancestry and left it at that, but it was clear that Potter had understood the word *Africain* and the table went silent.

When dessert was being served, René checked his watch and said that he had to get Lisette home. I told her that I guessed the story of my great fish would have to wait. She smiled as she shook my hand. "Perhaps you can tell me soon. I do not live far."

"You may borrow the Mercedes if that would help," René said, and then clucked for Babette to come out from underneath the table and wished us a good night.

After Lisette and René had left, Potter and I admitted that we only knew two Negroes: the man who worked at the fishmonger's in

Chestnut Hill who spread black shoe polish on his bald head rather than use a toupee, and Mr. Walsh, the local mailman. We agreed that it was kind of cool to be in a foreign country with a beautiful, dark-skinned woman, even if she wasn't really all that dark.

In the end, Potter wished me *bonne chance*, saying that the language barrier was too great for him and that he had his hands more than full with Sidney. I was relieved by Potter's comments and cupped my hands to jokingly acknowledge that Sidney's bodacious hogans were definitely a handful, but Potter didn't smile. He merely shook his head and said this time he wasn't kidding.

As I lay awake that night, I couldn't get it out of my mind how cavalier Potter was in his approach to girls and wondered what he'd meant about having his hands full with Sidney. The thought that some good had finally come from Potter's inability to speak French made me smile because it meant that I wouldn't have to compete with him for Lisette's attention, and I liked that—liked it a lot. I guessed I was what Mom would have called "smitten," and, as foreign as the feeling was, I liked that a lot, too.

Lisette

My first night with Lisette, we drove to a hillside that overlooked the lights of the town and beyond to the bay. Our view was blackened by low, heavy clouds, but I put down the top of the Mercedes anyway, and for a moment neither of us spoke. Finally, Lisette giggled. "*Ensuite?*"

I laughed too but couldn't think of anything else to say and asked if she was really eighteen.

"I will be," she said, "on July twenty-first. Perhaps you will bake me a cake?"

"I'm not so sure that's such a good idea," I said.

"Perhaps not." She smiled. "And when is your birthday? And why do you ask about mine?"

I said that I'd turned eighteen in January and had asked about her age because I wasn't sure if René wasn't stretching the truth a bit.

"My uncle?" She shook her head no. "He would never do that. He is different, yes, very different, but he is honest and caring. He is more of a father to me than my real father."

"Truly?"

Lisette hesitated. "Yes. My father is a very rough man. Filled with anger and drink."

"And your mom?"

"She took me from my father when I was a little girl." She turned away from me and stared out at the bay. "She died six years ago, and I live with my father once again."

"I'm sorry," I said. "Really sorry."

"I believe you," she said and turned back toward me. "And your parents? Are they gentle like you?"

"They're a bit old fashioned." I laughed. "That's an understatement. And my mom's got a drinking problem like your father, but in her own way she means well. They both have always been very good to me."

"You are fortunate." Lisette took a deep breath and smiled. "Enough seriousness. Tell me about Potter and living with a wealthy man like Monsieur Trudeau."

After I'd explained how I'd ended up with Potter and M. Trudeau, questions about each other came in rapid succession, both of us laughing and interrupting the other as we talked about how it felt to be out of high school, what our lives were really like, and how we'd like to see our futures. Lisette said that someday she'd like to get away from La Malbaie, perhaps move to Quebec City or Montreal, and start a family. I told her how excited I was to be going to college and admitted that I couldn't really think much beyond that.

Even though we had so little in common—other than we both had a parent who drank too much and older sisters whom we loved a lot—we couldn't learn enough about the other's background. We shared the same perspective on so many things, and while we teased about our differences, both realized that we'd found someone to confide in, someone removed enough from the other's life that being open and honest bore no risk. In my case, I'd found someone who didn't view my openness as a sign of weakness and with whom I didn't run the risk of a sarcastic reply.

When Lisette asked about my *grand saumon*, I told her of my disapproval of the fish being killed, that she had been carrying thousands of eggs that would produce more salmon to be caught someday; then I stopped when I realized that I was sharing a less than macho thought with a girl I'd just met and was trying desperately to impress. I was wondering what it was about her that let me speak so freely, when she pushed my shoulder playfully and said, "I know, Fran, I know. We Canadians kill all the fish we catch. Is there not a chance that someday they may all be gone? Then, you will have seen the future. You will be known as a prophet."

"Somehow I doubt it," I said, and we sat for a moment in silence, the breeze from the bay chilling us. I looked at the clock on the Mercedes's mahogany dash and said we'd better get home, that I had to be at the mill early the next morning.

Lisette nodded and smiled. "I understand, but could I offer you a kiss so you will come back to me?"

Although it wasn't my first kiss, it was my first *perfect* kiss, and it had its desired effect, because from that point on, Lisette and I spent every night together either in M. Trudeau's Mercedes or on the couch in my cabin, kissing and fighting the longing as best we could.

───※───

One morning, early the following week, as the sun crept over the horizon of La Malbaie, Potter knocked on my screen door and whispered, "Delafield, you awake?"

I grunted and waved him in. He was wearing his boxer shorts and had wrapped a blanket around his shoulders to protect him from the cool morning air. He sat at the foot of my bed, but for a moment he didn't speak. He ran a hand through his uncombed hair, and it seemed as though he was having trouble looking me in the eye when he said, "Delafield, we're leaving."

"You've got to be kidding," I said.

"Nope. We're out of here in a day or two. This isn't working out, and Dad and Mr. Trudeau agree."

I had known Potter since kindergarten—through grade school and high school—and knew he was lying. "Spill it," I said. "What's going on?"

He turned toward me and pulled the blanket tight across his chest. His eyes were bright with tears. "Sidney's pregnant."

"Holy shit! So that's what's behind all the phone calls."

All Potter could do was nod, and I asked if he was sure.

He nodded again. "We've been sweating it for almost a month."

I thought this had to be nothing more than a bad dream; I'd just started to date the most beautiful and carefree girl I'd ever met, I was being waited on hand and foot, was getting paid for doing next to nothing, and my friend was dragging me away from all of this just because he'd knocked up some round-heeled debutante with big tits?

I thought it wasn't just a bad dream, it was a goddamned nightmare. Then suddenly Potter's past flashed through my mind. We were finishing our seventh-grade year when our small class learned that he was having his testicles surgically lowered that summer. Of course we whispered and wondered about this mysterious surgical procedure, although I've never been quite sure how we learned it was going to happen. Nonetheless, that summer the surgical miracle took place, and when our classmates arrived back at school to begin our eighth-grade year, all twenty of us were overwhelmed by what we found: Potter was a man. More than a man, he was an instant he-man. He had grown at least half a foot and, what's more, was rugged looking with a deep voice and a dark beard, dark and heavy enough to shave almost every day. But it was more than his voice and beard that were so astonishing. It was the defined musculature of his body and the black, curly hair that covered it, and we all agreed that Potter looked more like a teacher in the showers than one of us.

On the next-to-last day of school, he gained even more stature within his circle of friends when he told us that the previous weekend he'd "gone all the way"—not once, but seven times—with an eighteen-year-old girl who up until that point had been his babysitter. Incredibly, Potter lost his virginity at thirteen, and, while I was impressed and envious of his newfound sexual prowess, I was a bit intimidated by it as well.

I took a deep breath, sat up, and asked if his parents knew.

"Are you shitting me?" Potter said. "Nobody knows but Sidney and me. And now you. And it's got to stay that way. Okay?"

I said he had my word on it and added that I was sorry.

"Jesus, Delafield," Potter shot back. "'Sorry' doesn't quite cover it."

To calm him a bit, I said it could be a false alarm.

"I sure as hell hope so," he said.

When I asked if there was a chance I could stay in La Malbaie, Potter quickly said no, and then apologized for the abruptness of his answer, adding that this was his old man's deal with Mr. Trudeau, and it included the two of us.

Then, for the first time, he looked directly at me and rested his hand on my shoulder. "I know I've been a shitty friend through all of this, Delafield, and I'm sorry to screw up your summer, but please don't complicate things any more than they already are." He choked back his tears. "What the hell do I do if it isn't a false alarm? Marry her? At eighteen? Quit Princeton before I even start? I'm in deep shit and need you to go along with me...on...on everything...because right now you're the only friend I've got."

Not knowing if what I was saying was the truth, I assured him that Sidney didn't want to get married any more than he did, that somehow, some way, everything was going to be okay. And then Potter Morris—the he-man whom all his friends had looked up to at thirteen, but now a scared kid of eighteen—wrapped his arms around my neck and bawled like a baby.

That night Lisette was subdued when I picked her up, and she asked me to take her directly to my cabin. As I drove, I chattered about my day at the mill while Lisette looked away, letting the wind blow her hair about her face, seeming not to hear a word I was saying.

Once inside the cabin, I sat on the couch and reached to pull her to me, but she clasped her hands behind her back and stepped away. She closed her eyes and shook her head. When she opened her eyes she said, "You are leaving, no?"

Again I reached for her hands, but again she refused me. "Who told you that?" I asked.

"My uncle. Is it true?"

I told her yes, it was true. I said that Potter had a family crisis in Philadelphia, and we would be leaving in two days' time. And I was very unhappy.

"But not unhappy enough to stay."

I tried to explain that I would stay if I could, but it wasn't my decision. "I am Potter's guest. His father's guest is more like it. Please try to understand."

She drew her hands from behind her back and gave me a hopeful look. "*So*, you would like to stay with me?"

"More than anything in the whole world," I answered.

"Truly?"

"Truly," I said. "I promise."

Lisette smiled, leaned forward and kissed me, and pulled me to my feet. At the bedroom door, she lowered the light from the Coleman lantern and drew my hands to the top button of her blouse and whispered, "Please, undress me."

We lay in each other's arms for a long while without speaking. Finally, Lisette asked if it was my first time. I thought about trying to make myself more grown up but ended up telling her the truth. "And you?"

"Couldn't you tell?"

I looked down at her and kissed her. A small silver cross on a thin chain rose and fell between her breasts. It was the only jewelry she wore, and I thought that any more would have marred her evenly colored skin and the soft curves and swells of her body. As inexperienced as I was in the ways of women, I knew that I was in the presence of an extraordinary beauty and thought that I could stay with her forever. "I'm glad it was with you," I said.

"It makes us very special," Lisette said and began to cry. "You are my prophet, remember? So what do you see in the future? I pray it is us." She wrapped her arms around my neck and pulled me to her. "Will you come back, Fran? For me?"

I promised that I would. It was a promise I desperately wanted to keep but didn't know if I could. I couldn't have predicted that any of this would happen, and I was confused by it all and had a hard time figuring out where I belonged. I thought in baseball terms that I was caught between bases and didn't know which way to turn.

"Twelve-Twelve"

On my first evening back home, I felt as though I was being held in purgatory while Mom fussed over dinner and Dad cooled off in the pool, swimming laps in his slow, mechanical Australian crawl. It wasn't until Mom had finished in the kitchen and Dad had mixed two old-fashioneds that they positioned themselves in the small Salterini loveseat on the terrace and said they were anxious to discuss my "abbreviated" visit to La Malbaie.

While my mother quizzed me about how much French I'd spoken, my father squeezed lighter fluid into his treasured Zippo, the one that bore a bold white *A* within a blue-and-red circle, the medallion of the Third Army. I should have known from his indifferent attitude that this wasn't going to be the most fun talk I'd ever had with him.

When he finished with his lighter, he lit a cigarette and took a long drag. "Bill Ames tells me that he ran into you at his fishing club in Quebec."

This piece of news relaxed me a bit, and I asked if Dr. Ames had told him about my big fish.

Dad nodded a number of times as though he was thinking about what to say next. "He also said you were with that Trudeau fellow's odd little man."

I was surprised that René might be the issue behind Dad's coolness and explained that he was nothing more than Potter's and my caretaker, mostly driving us to and from the mill and making sure that we were on time for breakfast and dinner.

"Oh?" My mother raised an eyebrow. "If you were being taken such good care of, why did you come home?"

I stuck to the script that Potter and I had rehearsed: the work wasn't as physical as we'd expected, and Potter had a difficult time at the mill because he didn't speak French.

Dad drew on his cigarette. "That's not what his father told me. He said this René character was as queer as Dick's hatband and gave Potter the creeps."

I thought, holy shit! What else had Potter said that we hadn't agreed on? But I decided it was best to stay with our story. "That's not exactly right, Dad," I said. "We were disappointed that all we did was sit all day at the mill, and Potter was surprised at how much French he needed to know. That's all there was to it. René really wasn't much of a factor."

"But it's still not clear," my mother said in French. "Why did you come home if it wasn't all that bad?" Asking in French was a little game Mom played with Heather and me. We thought she did it to stay one step ahead of Dad.

"You're right, Mom, it wasn't all that bad, but not at all what we expected or hoped for," I said. "We didn't really do anything. Didn't get any exercise. We just sat around all day in these noisy little rooms checking gauges. Potter's boss got frustrated with him because he couldn't speak French, and Potter decided he wasn't willing to put up with the arrangement for the entire summer. Simple as that."

Each of my answers and explanations was followed by another insinuating question, and I found myself getting angry at Mom and Dad, and at Potter too, who, as always, seemed to have given in to pressure from his father. "Dad, it's pretty simple," I said, trying to settle the issue once and for all. "It wasn't a lot of fun for Potter, and he decided that we should leave. He told me that his father and M. Trudeau agreed. When I asked if I could stay, Potter said I couldn't, that it was his father's deal, not ours."

"Huh?" Dad said. "That's it?"

"All of it," I said. "Believe me, there's nothing more."

Dad fumbled for another Pall Mall and lit it. "Well, okay, as long as you find a job here." He took a drag and blew smoke through his nose. "As an afterthought, Tom Morris also told me that he never really trusted Trudeau after he learned that he'd cut off his trigger finger to stay out of the war." He shook his head disapprovingly and chuckled. "Those French Canadians sound like an odd bunch to me."

Those French Canadians sound like an odd bunch? Did that include Lisette? I had wanted so badly to tell my parents about her and about my fishing trip and how kind Dr. Ames had been, but realized that the less I talked about La Malbaie, the better.

Potter called a few days later from Northeast Harbor to tell me that Sidney had gotten her period and that, as soon as he'd received the good news, he'd joined his parents in Maine, where he'd met a girl named Fiddle Mellon and planned to devote the rest of the summer to trying to get into her bloomers.

Frankly, I was incensed. Not only had Potter failed to hold up his end of the bargain on what we'd planned to say about La Malbaie, but all because of a false alarm, he'd ruined what promised to be the best summer of my life, and then he went about his selfish pursuits without ever offering me even the slightest apology.

The night of Potter's call, Heather and I sat shoulder to shoulder on the flagstone border to our swimming pool turning our feet in small circles in the water, and it didn't take long before I unloaded my anger. I began by saying that Potter was supposed to be my friend, but he'd kept Sidney a secret from me until he couldn't wait any longer and then lied to his father about me and La Malbaie.

"Jesus H. Criminy, Franny," Heather said, "doesn't anyone take precautions these days? There ought to be a section in the *Social Register* along with 'Married Maidens' devoted to shotgun marriages. Look what's happened to Jake Norris and Maggie Perry. Married in high school? They've got to be kidding!"

(Heather was referring to the son of one of our parents' friends who had gotten a sixteen-year-old girl pregnant and married her while he was a senior in school. It was the topic of many a cocktail hour, and our parents were so disapproving and talked about it so often that Heather and I assumed they were trying to send us a message.)

Heather leaned against me and patted my knee. "You being careful?"

"Of course," I said, although that first night with Lisette, things had happened so unexpectedly that I hadn't been prepared, but from that point forward I'd been careful and knew the odds were in my favor. Nonetheless, I felt a bit uneasy and quickly took the spotlight off of me and asked about her.

"Not to worry," Heather said, and kicked her feet in the water and giggled. "I have yet to meet the guy who's worthy of the honor." She paused. "So we're okay?"

"Yup," I assured her. "We're okay."

A Dilemma to End All Dilemmas

Within a week I began doing grunt work for a local builder to "earn my keep"—my father's words, not mine—and wrote Lisette daily. A few days before she turned eighteen, I sent her a birthday card, and on her birthday, I called her from a pay phone so the charge wouldn't show up on my parents' bill. After a few rings, her father answered, but when I asked to speak to her, he slurred a few Quebecois curses and hung up. He did the same on the second call, and I figured that, as badly as I wanted to hear her voice, there was no sense in calling again.

Almost a month passed, and my parents were getting ready to settle in for their cocktail hour when Mom called to me at the pool. "Fran, there's a girl named Lisette on the phone. She sounds very upset."

I ran to the living room and took the receiver from my mother. When I said hello, Lisette didn't answer, and I thought I could hear her choking back tears. I felt crowded by Mom, even though she stood a few paces from me, and I turned my back to her and asked

Lisette if she was okay. There was a long silence, and then she said, "I am going to have a child."

I thought she had to be kidding. That was Potter's story, not mine; this couldn't be happening to me. After a pause I said, "Just a minute," and asked Mom if she would hold the phone while I picked up in their bedroom. I took the stairs two at a time and thanked Mom once I was on the phone. I could hear Lisette sobbing as I waited for my mother to hang up, an event that seemed to take forever.

After a moment I said, "I'm here now."

"Are we alone?" Lisette asked.

"Yes. So, please, start over. You're pregnant?"

"Yes."

"You're sure?"

"I am certain. I talked to the doctor today."

After all the harsh judgments I'd made about Potter and Sidney, the shoe was now on the other foot. But I thought that my case was different. I was fond of Lisette. Maybe even in love with her. I enjoyed being with her more than any girl I'd ever known. Different as night and day.

"My God," I said, "what are you going to do?"

"I am going to have a baby."

While I waited for her to continue, I stared out the large bay window of my parents' bedroom but registered nothing.

"Our baby. Your baby."

Dark, resentful thoughts ran through my mind in an unsympathetic fashion. In an instant my whole life had been thrown into a cocked hat, and I was scared—really scared—for the first time in my adult life. It wasn't only the dilemma and its embarrassment that scared me; it was the disruption of how I'd hoped the next four years of my life would play out. I drew a deep breath and told Lisette that she had other choices.

"I do not think so," she said.

"But, Lisette, you're barely eighteen. How would you raise a child?"

"With you, Fran, as its father. Together."

The panicked feeling grew even more intense. "But I don't think you understand. I'm going to college in a few weeks. I can't raise a child and go to college too."

"But this is your child, Fran. Your responsibility."

"And partly my decision, as well?" I asked. "Because we do have other options. Difficult options, I know, but—"

"When we first met, you told me how upset you were when the guide killed your great fish," she said. "Imagine how you would feel if you let someone kill your child."

I was speechless; I felt trapped. Finally, I said, "But, Lisette, this is different."

"Not for me. Besides, it is against the law."

In frustration and confusion, I wrapped the receiver cord tight around my finger and asked in a challenging voice, "Then what are you proposing?"

Lisette didn't hesitate. "Getting married and raising our child. I will make you a good wife. That I promise."

"And if I can't say yes?"

"Then I will be alone and brokenhearted, and your child will be fatherless."

She spoke with such pain and gentleness that I wanted to reach through the phone and hold her. "Who knows about this?" I asked.

"The doctor and my sister. No one more. But I will not be able to keep it a secret for long."

I told her that I needed some time to think it through, that it was so unexpected.

"If you must," she said. "But I had hoped you would want to marry me because I want to marry you."

"But we're only eighteen," I said, "and I haven't even started college. It's not you, Lisette, it's the timing of it all."

"Perhaps, but we have no choice, and I know we can do it well. I will love you, Fran, forever."

I started to say something but could only cough out, "Ah, Lisette," and couldn't go on. No one had ever said such a thing to me. I told her that I'd call in a day or two. Before I could say anything more, she hung up.

I let out a deep breath and waited for my trembling to subside. I could hear Mom and Dad talking with Heather on the terrace below, and it occurred to me that I'd never really been in trouble as a kid, but all of a sudden here I was in *serious* trouble, and I had no idea what to do or who to turn to.

I started downstairs but stopped on the landing at the top of the stairs and debated if I should somehow try to keep this secret and convince Lisette to have things taken care of, or if I should level with my parents and seek their advice and, hopefully, their support.

As I tried to make sense of it all, to convince myself that my parents' reaction was secondary, I thought that Lisette would have the baby whether I married her or not. I didn't think I could live with that, and I headed down the stairs to face my parents, and my problem, like a man, the way Dad had always told me I should.

When I rejoined my family on the terrace, Heather was holding Dad's discarded copy of *The Evening Bulletin* in front of her as though she were shielding herself. She nodded at me and mouthed, "*En garde.*"

Mom spoke first. "Was that the girl you write every day? She sounded very upset."

As I tried to gather my thoughts—more accurately, my courage—all I could think of was the gentleness of Lisette's voice, saying that we had no choice, that we could do it well, that she would love me forever. A tall order, but I wanted so badly to believe her, and blurted out, "Yes, Mom, she's the girl. Her name is Lisette Jaud. She's eighteen and is pregnant with my child and wants to marry me."

Before either of my parents could respond, Heather lowered the newspaper and said, "And she's colored, weighs four hundred pounds, has syphilis and only one leg, and—"

Things were spinning out of control, and I waved my hands to interrupt her. To stop her. "This is no joke."

Heather looked startled and pulled back in her chair. "Franny? You're not serious? After our…"

No one spoke.

Mom and Dad looked at one another, and Dad took a sip of his drink, followed by a long drag on his cigarette.

Again, it was Mom who spoke first. "Of course you told her that she must get it taken care of. *N'est pas?*"

When I said no, that I'd told Lisette I needed some time to think about what we should do, Mom looked at my father and said, "Theo? A little help here, please. He is your responsibility, too."

Dad closed his eyes for a second. "There's nothing to think about, Fran. You tell that little tramp she must get her situation fixed and you will pay whatever it takes." He paused. "But only if you're sure you're the father." He paused again. "Well, are you?"

I said I was.

"How can you be sure?"

"Because Lisette wouldn't lie to me, and, for future reference, Dad, she's not a tramp, and she won't do what you're suggesting."

"My mistake," Dad said.

Mom smirked. "This Lisette, who is not a tramp, what does she do? And does she speak English? She spoke to me in French, if you can call it that."

I said she was the town telephone operator and admitted that she only spoke a few words of English.

"Good God, Fran, will you listen to yourself?" my father said. "I know it's difficult for you to accept, but this girl saw you living with the richest man in town and assumed that you too must be wealthy and created a situation—at least says she has—that forces you to marry her. I can assure you that this isn't about principles. It's about money."

"But, Dad, you've never even met her and you're accusing—"

"Women of the lower classes are always trying to better themselves, regardless of cost," my mother interrupted. She gave Dad a pointed look. "Isn't that right, Theo?"

"Your mother's right, of course," he said and looked away for a moment. "Women like this were a dime a dozen in Europe during the war. It's the oldest ploy in the books. Offer to pay her five thousand dollars to make the problem go away and see what she says then."

"And if she says no?" I asked.

"Don't worry, she won't. You'll see. I know the drill."

I had no idea if my father was right, but I became uneasy as I remembered that Lisette had said she wanted to move away from La Malbaie someday and start a family, and how she had led me to the bedroom that first night and asked me to undress her, and how eager she was to sleep with me a second time. For a moment I wondered—and later hated myself for it—if I *had* been set up, if Lisette's plea that she would end up alone and brokenhearted and her child fatherless was simply a negotiating ploy. I tried to convince myself that my fears were unwarranted and said, "And if you're wrong, Dad?"

"Then skip all this nonsense and marry her, Franny," Heather said. "And, Mom and Dad, don't think for a moment that if I were in her position I'd risk an abortion, because you can bet your sweet bippy I wouldn't."

"Heather, please, not now," my father said.

"Why not?" she asked. "Isn't it helpful to have another young woman's perspective?"

Dad raised his hands in mock surrender. "Of course, but there's a lot going on here right now, Heather, so please stay out of this. I'll hear what you have to say later."

For a long, uncomfortable moment, all were quiet. Finally, Mom muttered Dad's name, her hand trembling as she handed him her empty cocktail glass. He stood, took the glass, and walked to the bar in the dining room as though he'd been defeated by something.

There was another awkward pause until Mom asked, "Do you love this girl? Have you met her parents?"

"I loved her when we were together, but having been separated for a while, I'm not sure anymore," I said. "Shouldn't absence make the heart grow fonder? Did it for you and Dad during the war? And can being deprived of things you really want stop you from loving someone as much as you once thought you did?"

Mom looked to see if Dad was listening and lowered her voice. "Circumstances do affect your emotions, and, yes, things changed for a lot of people during the war." She paused. "And after. But this is a different kind of war—one that many men have fought and lost—and it is now your war. You started it, so you must end it."

Desperate for her support, I asked if she would help me.

She chose not to answer. Instead, she said, "You didn't tell me if you've met the girl's parents."

"I've said hello to her father. Her mother died when she was twelve."

"And what does her father do?"

"What does that matter?" Heather asked.

"Heather, *doucement!*" Mom snapped.

"He works in the mill," I said, and thought, "And he's a mean drunk most of the time," but I didn't think that would be a good thing for Mom to hear. Besides, I still wanted to know if I had any allies in this new war of mine. "But you didn't answer *my* question, Mom. Will you help me?"

My mother stared at me for a long time as though she was carefully weighing her answer. She wiped tears from her cheeks, stubbed out her cigarette, and shook her head. "I don't know how

I can. You will tarnish the Delafield name if you do what this girl is asking. And if that's the case, I cannot help. You have put yourself in this familiar mess, and now it's up to you to get out of it. I'm sure it's nothing more than a teenage infatuation based on sex and will pass in time. That's usually the way it goes, no matter what age you men are."

"Would you feel differently if she was rich?" I asked.

Mom smirked. "Money doesn't mean a thing, Fran; breeding means everything." She stood uncertainly and walked inside to serve dinner, taking her old-fashioned from Dad as they passed in the doorway.

My mother. My mom. The one I thought might show some understanding, maybe even some sympathy, but she'd let me down when I needed her most. I tried to give her the benefit of the doubt because this was the first time she'd had to address an adult problem with me. No more scraped knees. No more scraps with Heather. This was the real deal: a girl she'd never met, whose parents she didn't know, was pregnant and insisted on marrying her only son, the only one who could carry on the good Delafield name.

When I looked up, Dad beckoned for Heather and me to come in and get our dinner. He placed a hand gently on my shoulder as I passed him, confusing me even further.

Once in the dining room, I could hear my mother sobbing in the kitchen and saying, "Talk about déjà vu." But, when she finally joined us at the table, it was as though nothing had happened. Nothing had changed. My family sat, Dad nodded at us, and we all bowed our heads and repeated, "Bless, oh Lord, this food to our use, and us to thy loving service, and keep us ever mindful of the wants and needs of others. Amen."

Ever mindful of the wants and needs of others? And Dad had asked me to listen to *myself*?

He couldn't be serious. Mom couldn't be serious. Was all this stuff that they preached and recited nothing more than a reflex?

Did they know what the words they were saying really meant? Were they parenting me or just going through the paces, the tried-and-true paces, avoiding the really rough spots? And what about me? Was I doing the same with Lisette? All new questions, and I hadn't a clue what any of the right answers were.

A War of Attrition

As I was certain she would, Lisette refused to take the $5,000. While I told her, over and over, that it was my father's idea, that I'd made the offer only to prove that money was not what she was after, she was hurt and offended by the offer. "But deep in your heart, were you hoping that I would take it?" she asked. "You may tell me the truth, Fran. I know this is very difficult for you."

I said that I hated the idea of bribing her to do something she was so strongly against and wanted to prove to my parents how wrong they were about her. What I didn't say was that getting married and becoming a father was not the way I'd envisioned my years at Dartmouth and that, yes, there were moments when I'd hoped she would take the money and make the whole problem disappear. But as I talked with her, she was so understanding, so quick to trust me, that I was reminded how much I cared for her. Finally I said, "What I hope is…is that we can make this work." And it was with that sentiment—*I hope we can make this work*—that I committed to marrying Lisette, not only because I felt it was the honorable thing to do, but because I was convinced that I loved her.

My parents were horrified by my "impetuous, childish decision" and instantly set up strict parameters going forward. "First," my father said, "if you're going to do something as foolish as marry some eighteen-year-old whom you barely know, your mother and I will sanction it only if you carry out your plans to get your degree. If you won't, we won't lay out another—"

"I'm afraid I already know the answer to this question," I interrupted, "but is there no way you can show a little sympathy... or understanding...or something...for my situation? Maybe even give me a little support for my decision?"

When my father answered that they were supporting me by sending me to Dartmouth, I abandoned all hope and challenged him for the first time in my life. "Is everything about money and nothing else, Dad? You don't get it, do you? I'm not talking about financial support. I'm asking for—*pleading* for—you and Mom to help me get through this."

Dad glanced at my mother, who looked away. He said, "Our concession is that...that this girl—"

"It's Lisette, Dad," I said. "It's not really that hard to remember."

"That if you don't see the light and actually go through with this," he continued, "Lisette will live with us, at least until the baby is born."

"And," my mother added, "if you don't change your mind and anyone asks, we'll say we're doing a Canadian friend a favor by looking after their daughter while she has her child out of wedlock."

I couldn't believe what I was hearing. I was discouraged; more than discouraged—defeated. "And when the baby's born, then what?"

"We'll cross that bridge when...and *if*...we have to," Dad said. "Perhaps you'll be able to work out something with Dartmouth by then. If not, you'll have to make some major changes. This is a short-term solution at best."

"And one we hope will never come to pass," my mother said. Then, without giving me a chance to ask what "making major changes" might mean, she asked, "This child, will you raise it a Catholic?"

I told her that I hadn't thought that far ahead but that I'd do whatever Lisette wanted.

"You certainly are willing to make large concessions to this Lisette," Mom said and lit a cigarette. "I take it from that that our only grandchild will be a Catholic."

I said I guessed that's what would happen.

"Oh, Fran," my mother said. "This is just what your Huguenot ancestors tried to escape."

Dad looked at her as though he now was seeking her approval. "And one other thing, Fran. About the wedding. It's a long drive and would be expensive to fly and rent a car. And besides…" He paused.

I waited for him to continue. When he chose not to say what he had started to say, I said that there was no chance they'd be seen at the wedding by anyone who knew them, and pleaded with them to come.

Mom snapped back, "Fran, you don't seem to understand, and I don't blame you because your father's not being direct with you. The fact is we won't dignify such an affair with our presence."

I knew at that point that I'd never be able to overcome my parents' disapproval. More importantly, I finally understood that I'd never be able to do anything to relieve their shame. But at the same time, rather than trying to understand and be sympathetic to their feelings, I wondered why I should try to meet them halfway if they weren't willing to do the same.

During the next few days, I became overwhelmed by their cold greetings, our numerous disagreements, and their frequently repeated mandates, all of which caused me to wonder if I shouldn't just say to hell with Dartmouth, go to Canada, marry Lisette, and make some kind of a life there.

It was Heather who encouraged me to give Mom and Dad's plan a try, at least for a semester, before making such a dramatic move. "But it doesn't make any sense," I said. "It's nothing more than a waiting game."

"And that's the brilliance of it, Franny," Heather said. "*You* think it only prolongs the inevitable. *They* see it as a war of attrition. I'll bet they think that when you leave for Dartmouth, Lisette will have her pregnancy taken care of, or take Dad's five thousand dollars and leave, or both."

"She would never do that," I said.

"You're sure?" Heather said.

I nodded.

"Then just let it play out. Plenty of guys have ended up as young fathers in college and have found a way to make it work."

Reluctantly, when Heather made it clear what game our parents were playing, I accepted her advice, mainly because it was a compromise that offered me the best of both worlds and would, I hoped, eventually prove Mom and Dad wrong. So terribly wrong.

Soon after my talk with Heather, in one of my many phone calls with Lisette (sometimes there were three, even four a day), I learned that things weren't going any better for her than they were for me. The priest in La Malbaie had refused to marry us because I wasn't a Catholic, and it had taken a lot of work on Lisette's part to convince the local justice of the peace to conduct the proceeding. On top of that, in a drunken rage, her father had called her as big a whore as her mother and said he was glad to be rid of her.

When I reported these frustrations to my parents (admittedly in a very watered-down form), Mom burst into tears. "Oh my God, what kind of people have you gotten involved with? Don't do it, Fran," she said. "For God's sake, and our family's sake, don't do it."

Mom's tearful plea aside, all of this convinced me that it was my job as Lisette's future husband to free her from La Malbaie, something that she often pleaded with me to do. I thought it was an important first step if we were to have a chance of being happy.

What's more, maybe it was because we were frightened and confused eighteen-year-olds, or maybe it was no more complicated than we were truly in love, but the angry insults from Lisette's father, and my parents' mandates, stiffened our resolve.

When I announced that we'd set our wedding date for September tenth, Mom said, "Saturday, the tenth? Isn't that the night of the Wolcotts' party for Emily?"

I said it was, that I'd write Mr. and Mrs. Wolcott a letter sending them my regrets.

"But, Fran," my mother said, "that party means so much to Bob and Nancy. They're even having Louis Armstrong play at dinner."

I tried to tell her that I understood how important debutante parties were to her and her friends. I added that I'd attended a tea, or a dinner and a dance, or a dinner-dance from the day I'd graduated from school until the end of June and thought I could miss a few in September.

Mom drew her purse close to her and fumbled through it. Her hands seemed palsied as she studied the pages of her small, red-leather-bound date book. "And what about Barbara Wainwright's party on the seventh, and Sally Sargent's on the thirteenth? What will you do about those?"

"I'm getting married, Mom. Soon. Remember? So please try to understand: I won't be going to any more deb parties."

"Oh," she said. "Not even the Assembly?"

I thought it was time to try to force Mom to accept how my life—and hers and Dad's—was about to change. In as gentle a tone as I could muster, I said, "Not even the Assembly." While I suddenly felt a sense of independence when I said it, at the same time, I worried about what I was leaving behind: friends, a way of life I'd grown to accept, the familiarity of it all.

"But the Assembly is Philadelphia's oldest..." She paused for a moment, glanced at Dad, and then stared at me. Her anger pushed through her confusion and resignation. "Good God, Francis, you've ruined everything. The least you could do is go to Barbara Wainwright's party before…before you get…" She took a cigarette from her purse and forced it to her lips. She tried to steady her lighter and then snapped it shut and dropped it and the cigarette back in her purse. "I can't even say it. I can't even say it, Fran. I've never been so ashamed."

After dinner, Heather and I sat shoulder to shoulder at the edge of the pool, as always idly stirring our feet in the water. Neither of us spoke for quite a while until Heather said, "I miss the fireflies, Franny."

When I asked her what the heck she was talking about, I realized that she was crying.

"I don't know. I miss the way things used to be, the way they were earlier in the summer before all this nasty crap began. I hate it. Absolutely hate it. I hate it for you, and I hate the way Mom and Dad have handled it."

I apologized for my part in all of it, said there are always two sides to everything.

Heather sniffled and said that I'd been patient as hell with Mom and Dad. "Not perfect, but close to it," she said and then added, "The trouble is, Mom was born a whole frigging century too late. And old Jim Beam isn't helping."

"That's all fine and dandy," I said, "but what do I do now?"

"A peace offering is worth a try," Heather said. "Why not go to Bar Wainwright's party to see if that would help?" She paused and lit a cigarette. "No matter how hard you try, or I try, we'll never really be free from our tribal heritage. So what's one more deb party in the cosmic order of things if it'll make Mom happy? It won't bring the fireflies back, Franny, but it can't hurt."

A Life Lesson

Three nights before I was to be married, I put on the tuxedo that had become my summer vacation uniform. Mom had, in her inimitable fashion, added her sense of style to my outfit by needle pointing a cummerbund that featured the Delafield family crest. She also insisted that I wear a black dinner jacket even in the hottest summer evenings because, as she put it, "Those white dinner jackets with their shawl collars are so nouveau."

As I made one final check in the mirror, it occurred to me that this would be the last time I'd wear a tuxedo—something that had become so much a part of my life, for better or for worse—for a long, long time, if ever again. My resentment of the unfairness of my dilemma and my parents' lack of support somewhat suppressed an uneasy feeling of nostalgia, perhaps even a sense of loss, that began to nag at me. And I wondered if Heather had been right about our inability to rid ourselves of our past.

Our upbringing.

A little after seven o'clock, I was greeted by a swarm of red-jacketed men who ran from one car to the next, trying to keep up with the steady stream of arrivals at the Wainwrights' manicured estate on the Main Line. After I'd surrendered the family Plymouth, I followed a stooped, red-faced man and his chatty, white-haired wife through the house to the receiving line where Barbara and her parents greeted their guests.

I paused for a moment and drew a deep breath, trying to shift into my mannerly gear. It was kind of a reflex action, like a prize fighter still fending off punches while out on his feet, but it helped me momentarily push aside my anger at my parents and my conflicting thoughts about tuxedos and debutantes. But, as I waited my turn to say hello, I imagined my mother sitting on our small terrace reading to Heather and me *The Evening Bulletin* society editor's predictable column that would say something like, "As the short, fall debut season neared its close, many will remember the lovely debutante Barbara Wainwright's party as a triumph. The Lester Lanin Orchestra, even Lester himself, seemed energized by the elegant setting of Maral Brook and the beautiful floral decorations that added just the right touch of color to the snow-white three-pole tent..."

When my turn came to greet Bar and Mrs. Wainwright, I did so with perfunctory kisses and some small talk but avoided discussing the painful topic of my last baseball game at ES with Mr. Wainwright, an Andover alum. We were playing at Andover and, going into the bottom of the ninth inning, not only were we leading 1–0, but I'd retired the first twenty-four batters I'd faced in order. Aware that I had a chance for a no-hitter—maybe even a perfect game—from the sixth inning on, my teammates stopped talking to me. Even Potter stopped his glove pounding and his incessant "Hum, you rock, you chuck, you Delafield babe," from his position at third base. After two quick outs, Andover's last hope took two called strikes, and everybody stood, Andover fans included, applauding and yelling for me to finish my perfect game. I massaged the ball to settle my nerves and looked at Potter, who was crouched, his elbows resting on his knees, his head bowed. For all I knew, Potter was praying.

I jammed the Andover hitter with my first pitch, and he hit a weak ground ball toward third base. Potter fielded the ball cleanly and then—I can still see it in slow motion as though it happened yesterday—as Potter cocked his arm to make his throw, the ball slipped from his hand and floated in a lazy arc and dropped with deadly silence on the grass behind him. At first he looked at me, frozen in disbelief, and turned to his left searching for the ball and then turned the other way and pounced on it, but the hitter had already rounded first base and, taking advantage of Potter's confusion, beat his throw to second.

What promised to be the high-water mark of my baseball career had been ruined, but the drama didn't end there. Reverend Crawford, the coach and our Latin teacher, jogged to the pitcher's mound and told me to walk Andover's next batter, saying that first base was already open and that I should pitch to the hitter that followed him, who was far less of a threat.

The Andover batter whom Mr. Crawford wanted me to walk was their shortstop, a guy by the name of Skip Fairburn, one of the best players in New England—so good, in fact, that the Red Sox were scouting him. After Fairburn had settled into the batter's box and worked his cleats into the dirt, my catcher stood, took a step to his right, and called for the first intentional ball.

Fairburn stepped out of the box and stared at me and then at Potter and muttered, "Episcopal pussies." When Potter heard Fairburn's comment, he yelled, "Delafield, wait up!" and hurried to the mound. He and Fairburn had competed for a girl from St. Timothy's—almost getting into a fight at a dance at the Marblehead Yacht Club the previous summer—and the girl had chosen Fairburn, something that no girl had ever done to Potter before, and he was still pissed off about it. He took the ball from me and said, "You can get this faggot," and slammed the ball back into my glove. "I know you can. Strike the son of a bitch out."

I took a deep breath and thought Potter was right, that I should go after Fairburn to prove that this was *my* game. Without a shadow of a doubt my game. I picked up the rosin bag and shook off my catcher's signs, signaling that I wanted to pitch.

The battle of wills between me and Fairburn continued until I'd run the count to 3–2. When the next pitch left my hand, I knew it didn't have the zip I'd hoped for, and Fairburn crushed it for a game-winning home run, and for all I know, the ball might still be rolling beyond the fence in left field if a golden retriever hadn't scooped it up and run away with it.

Partway through the bus ride back to school, Reverend Crawford curled his finger at me, inviting me to sit with him. He had changed from his coach's uniform to his clerical collar, and I sensed that we were going to talk about things other than baseball. "We play sports at Episcopal for many reasons," the reverend said. "One is *nosce te ipsum*, to know thyself. You're a bright and talented young man, Fran, but at times you let your emotions and your friends' wishes overtake the sensible thing to do. So do yourself a favor, and in the future, think at least twice before you leap." He patted my knee. "Okay?"

I nodded. "I'm sorry, sir."

"You don't have to apologize to me," he said. "It's your teammates you let down. And yourself. So I hope you've learned something from this."

I said I hoped that I had, too, and stood to go back to my seat when Reverend Crawford said, "So remember, Fran, occasionally in life you've got to give people an intentional pass to win the game."

"Yes, sir," I said. "Got it."

The reverend was smiling when he said, "I'll pray that you have."

"Good Night, Ladies"

Once I finished with the receiving line, I worked my way to the bar where I could order any drink I wanted, even though I was—as were the majority of the partygoers—under Pennsylvania's legal drinking age. During the long wait for dinner, I sought out Potter, who'd just returned from a foggy Labor Day weekend in Northeast Harbor. We huddled in a corner of the tent, removed from the din of the two hundred or so guests, where we could catch up. At first I approached the topic of La Malbaie tentatively, but after I'd drained the second bourbon and ginger and ordered a third, I couldn't keep it together any longer and asked Potter exactly what it was he'd told his father about why we left.

Potter said they talked about it before he'd learned that Sidney wasn't pregnant, and his father had backed him into a corner. He gave me an apologetic smile. "I guess I went off our script a little bit."

"A little bit?" I said.

"Okay. More than a little. I'm sorry, Delafield, but my old man was really on my case."

"But what the hell did you tell him about René?" I asked. "Dad implied that he and I were buddy-buddy, if you know what I mean."

"All I said was that René was a little light in his loafers. I never linked the two of you. I promise." He patted me on the shoulder. "Okay?"

"I guess, but damn, Potter, you should have warned me." I set my empty glass on the silver tray a waiter held in front of me and asked for another.

"Drowning your sorrows over Lisette?" Potter asked.

At that point I was almost drunk enough to tell Potter my whole story—almost drunk enough, but not quite, even though I was tempted. "Nah," I said. "My parents have given me a lot of shit since I've been home, and I'm ready to go to Hanover. Plenty ready."

Potter apologized again and tapped my glass. "Take it easy with the brown stuff. You're already halfway to being shit faced, and it's going to be a long night."

"Up yours," I said. "It's already been a long night."

When dinner was announced, I found myself flanked by Maisie Bingham, Bar Wainwright's roommate from Miss Porter's School, on my right, and Bar's fifteen-year-old brother on my left. I hadn't exactly drawn the seat of honor; I was mostly a houseguest-sitter and babysitter and was sure that no one would have missed me if I hadn't come at all, and I wondered how, exactly, I'd gotten myself into this mess.

But Maisie proved to be more than a run-of-the-mill debutante dinner partner. She had a good sense of humor, and, while she wasn't what Mom would call a classic beauty, she had a pretty spray of freckles that covered her nose and cheeks, was athletically built, and had an inviting smile and large blue eyes that matched her dress, giving her quite a lot of sex appeal. (I reluctantly admit that I do remember Maisie's dress not because of its color but because it fell open whenever she leaned forward, and she was the first girl I'd ever known who didn't wear a bra.)

My conversation with her wasn't what I expected either. Unlike most girls I'd just met, she didn't play the "who do you know?" game. Instead she wanted to talk about music (she loved Ray Charles and Bill Haley and thought Lester Lanin was a creep) and about movies (Marlon Brando and James Dean were her kind of guys). But what seemed to capture her imagination the most were photographs; photographs that told a story or captured someone's personality, or both. She told me that the images of Marilyn Monroe's skirt billowing over a subway grate and a picture in *Life* magazine of a sea of people in a movie theater wearing 3-D glasses were indelibly imprinted on her mind. "How great are they?" she asked.

When the endless stream of toasts was finally finished and Bar's brother had excused himself and slipped outside the tent where his parents couldn't see him sneak a smoke, Maisie turned to me as though she'd been waiting for him to leave. She smiled and drew a cigarette from a small evening purse and handed me her lighter. "And what did *you* do this summer, little boy?"

I said that I'd worked in a paper mill in Quebec.

"Was that fun?" she asked.

"It was okay."

"So you must speak French."

I said yes, I did.

"I'm jealous," she said. "I took French at Farmington for four years and can't speak a word. It was nothing but grammar and reading, a total waste of time."

I said I understood and explained that my mother was French and that I had a very good teacher at Episcopal.

"Lucky you."

I agreed and lit her cigarette and asked what she had done during the summer.

"Me? This summer?" She smiled, glanced at the others at the table to make sure they weren't listening and leaned close to me, blowing smoke toward my ear. "This summer, Francis Delafield, I discovered fucking."

I thought, "What a great answer," for I'd done the same, and laughed. "Was that fun?"

She ran a sharp fingernail the length of my thigh and giggled. "I'll bet it was more fun than working in a paper mill. You should give it a try sometime."

I grabbed her hand and looked directly at her. Her blue eyes were bright with excitement, her face flushed, the color spreading to her neck and chest. "So I've heard," I said.

She dug her fingernail in deeper and drew it slowly up my thigh. "As they say, there's no time like the present."

I lifted her hand and placed it on the table. "Sorry, but I'm already spoken for."

Maisie giggled and squeezed my hand. "Very funny, Fran. You're cute. Really cute." She reached for her glass. "Another, please?"

I struggled to my feet, and, as I turned to head for the bar, Maisie pulled on the back of my dinner jacket. I leaned toward her, steadying myself with a hand on the back of her chair. Her dress had fallen open again, and our faces were no more than a few inches apart. Her eyes followed mine to her breasts, and she smiled up at me. "Drop that spoken-for nonsense. You can look *and* touch. You won't be sorry you did."

Midnight approached, and Lester Lanin began to hand out his signature hats—purple, orange, red, blue, and yellow—and spurred his orchestra on as they dug into "When the Saints Go Marching In." From the stag line, I watched the dance floor fill and the energy level of the partygoers rise while I searched for Maisie. When I spotted her, I inched my way through the dancers to cut in. The minute I reached for her hand, she pulled me tight to her and pressed her cheek against mine and nipped at my earlobe. "Ready to compare me to the paper mill?"

Well down the steep, sweeping lawn, far from the lights of the tent, seated on a stone bench in the cover of a low-hanging willow, Maisie turned her back to me and asked me to zip her up. Suddenly, while I fumbled in the dark with her zipper, I was overcome with guilt and thought of the night Lisette had asked me to undress her. I was ashamed of what I'd just done and quickly pulled Maisie's zipper to a close.

She reached over her shoulder and held my hand in place and asked if I had a cigarette. When I told her that I didn't smoke, she said that was okay and paused. "You know…you know most guys your age are just 'wham, bam, thank you, ma'am,' but you screw like you've had some practice, like a married man."

I couldn't help but laugh. "You haven't done it with a—"

She took my hand from her shoulder and turned toward me. "That's what got me started. He was twenty-six, and I was babysitting for his two kids in Watch Hill. It started the first night he drove me home. He asked if he could kiss me good night. I thought he meant a little peck on the cheek, but when he took my face in his hands…well…it was so daring and exciting and fun. But after a while, he began to worry that his wife suspected something and dropped me like I never existed. Wouldn't even talk to me. But I was hooked, totally hooked." Her expression was cloaked in the darkness when she asked, "So? How was I?"

I'm sure I slurred my answer a bit. "You'd have made my mother happy. Very, very happy."

"What kind of an answer is that?" Maisie asked.

"You're the right kind of girl for my parents," I told her. "A Bingham, went to Farmington, lives in Greenwich, on your way to Bennett, all the proper stuff. All the boxes checked. It'd be okay with my mom if…if…if I got *you* pregnant."

"You worried about that?"

"Shit yes," I said. "Everybody who puts out these days gets knocked up."

Maisie rested her hand on my back and patted me like a child. "Not to worry, Fran. You're okay. I don't go anywhere without my trusty diaphragm."

"You think I'm okay?" I said. "What the hell do you know about being okay?"

"Easy, Fran," she said. "I don't know much about anything, but I think when you're sober, you're better than okay. Lots better. But right now you're nothing but drunk. Really angry about something and good and drunk." She stood, smoothed her hands down her dress, and fluffed her hair. "I look all right?"

"You look just fabulous," I said and began singing with the faraway music, "Good night, ladies, ladies, good night. It's time to say—"

"Fran, seriously, do I look okay enough to go back up there, or am I too much of a mess?"

I stopped singing and stood and struggled to pull on my dinner jacket. "No one will ever know that you've been fucking in the bushes, if that's what you mean." I pulled her hard against me and tried to kiss her.

She pushed me away and then reached to steady me. "Be nice," she said, squeezing my hands hard to hold me in place. "And don't treat me like a slab of beef or some whore. And be serious for a minute." She pulled me closer to her. "Please, Fran."

I apologized and told her that I was all mixed up. "Fucked up but good. Just because you fit the preppy mold doesn't mean you're not..." I stopped, not knowing what I would say next.

"Not what?"

I wrapped my arms around her and said, "I don't know." We stayed that way for a long time, neither of us speaking, just swaying to the distant strains of music. When I loosened my grasp, Maisie pulled me to her again and said, "A minute more, please, Fran. I like this part best of all."

I thought I liked it, too, and was confused as hell. I felt that I'd betrayed Lisette—been unfaithful to her—and I let go of Maisie and was wandering across the lawn toward the house and the red-jacketed men who had parked my car when she called out, "Hey, wait! Wait up. Where are you going?"

"To La Malbaie, to get married."

Maisie yelled back, "Fran, in English, please. What are you doing? I thought we were friends. You're not leaving me, are you?"

"I'm afraid so. Maybe in another life, but right now I'm going home." I added in French, "And I pray to God that I'm doing the right thing and that Mom and Dad are wrong. Dead fucking wrong."

Ma Femme

Heather and I arrived in La Malbaie just before dark. We'd driven all day in a car that Heather had borrowed from a friend, and I was on edge, but who wouldn't be at eighteen and about to get married against his parents' will? After we checked into L'Auberge de la Mer, the least expensive lodging in town, I settled into my room and called Lisette.

When Lisette arrived, my nerves and self-consciousness must have been on full display, and I would have been lost without Heather. She immediately embraced Lisette, telling how her how thrilled she was to finally have a sister, and tried to explain that I wasn't always such a *bouffon*, that I was just a nervous bridegroom. Before she excused herself for the night, she hugged Lisette again and said, "I think he'll be better in the morning." She laughed. "If he isn't, God help us all."

My small room smelled of Lysol and was sparsely equipped, lighted only by a yellow bulb in the lamp on the bedside table. I sat with Lisette at the end of one of the beds, and each of us waited for the other to speak. At one point we leaned forward to kiss but stopped and looked at each other and then looked away. After another uncomfortable period of silence, Lisette took my hand

and began to cry. "Are you here because you love me or because it is your duty? I know what type of man you are, Fran, so please be honest with me."

I was speechless because I wasn't sure what the answer was. I simply didn't know—or couldn't uncover—the truth. Why *was* I doing this? Really? Because I was madly in love and wanted to make this girl my lifelong partner? Or because it was the honorable, gentlemanly thing to do, the type of thing that was expected of boys with my upbringing? Or because I wanted to prove to my parents how narrow minded and wrong they were, and that—with or without them—I could stand on my own two feet?

Maybe it was all of the above. I wasn't sure, and I felt trapped because there was no way out of this dilemma, no turning back now. But long ago I'd realized that no one had ever believed in me as much as Lisette did, and I turned her toward me, mustered my courage, knowing full well the implications of what I was about to say, and told her that I was there because I wanted her to be my wife and the mother of my child.

She stared at me as though she was weighing my answer. Before she could speak, I kissed her eyes and said that I was there because I wanted to be, not because I had to be.

"Your sister feels the same?" she said.

"Couldn't you tell? She's my—our—biggest supporter," I said. "She will be a great friend to you. Just you wait and see."

"And your parents?"

"They will be difficult, my mother in particular. I cannot promise you otherwise."

"But you are going to try to make our marriage work?"

I said no, that our marriage *was* going to work.

"And the baby? Are you looking forward to becoming a father?"

It was the one question I'd avoided addressing because the idea was so foreign to me. I said I only hoped I would be a good father, and promised to try.

"Please, never forget what you have said tonight," Lisette said. "I am happy, and tomorrow I will commit to you for life." She kissed me lightly as though she was signing off on our conversation. Once again her eyes filled with tears, and the kiss that followed was as viscous and searching as any I had ever experienced. When she pulled away, blood trickled from a small split on her lower lip. "I will make you a good wife, Fran," she promised. "That I know."

The marriage ceremony began a little after eight the following morning in the cramped and stuffy office of La Malbaie's local *juge de paix,* who seemed to be in a hurry to get the distasteful task behind him and rushed through the formalities, completing all in less than ten minutes. The witnesses were Heather; Lisette's sister, Caroline; and René, who held Babette in the crook of his arm and who reminded me—not once but several times—that he was the one who had introduced me to my wife.

Immediately after Lisette and I had signed a few documents, we hurried to the car with Heather and began the long drive home, arriving in Chestnut Hill at dusk only to find the garage empty. I was furious and embarrassed but kept it to myself because I didn't want to make a potentially bad situation for Lisette any worse. Mom and Dad knew full well when we would be home, and I couldn't help thinking what a hostile welcoming this was, that things might be even more unpleasant for Lisette than I'd imagined. I dreaded the time she would spend living with them unless they changed their behavior and their feelings, something that I should have known would never happen.

The three of us settled in on the terrace and began an anxious wait for Lisette's new mother- and father-in-law to appear. Heather and she talked as though they'd known each other for years, while I paced back and forth, for some reason feeling like a child who was about to confess to a wrongdoing. I stopped my pacing when I heard Mom and Dad's voices in the hallway. Heather stood and grabbed Lisette's hand. "You will be fine," she said, and laughed and hugged her. "The good news is, Dad won't understand a word you say."

When we filed into the living room, it was empty.

Empty.

I could hear my parents talking upstairs and then heard a door close and heard Mom call to Dad. Heather and I exchanged confused looks, and just as Lisette asked if something was wrong, my father walked slowly into the living room and stopped in an awkward, wooden pose. Oddly, and totally out of character (at least I thought so at the time), when Dad saw Lisette, barefoot, wearing the white dress she'd worn at the ceremony with a sprig of purple and white wildflowers still in her hair, he drew a breath and stammered as though he was talking to some unseen companion. "My God, but she's beautiful," he said. He quickly looked at me and then Heather. "Your mother isn't feeling well and has gone to bed. She said to tell Lisette that she was sorry, that she would meet her in the morning."

From behind Dad, Heather raised a hand to her mouth and tipped an imaginary glass. I tried to shrug it off, for I had far more pressing matters than my mother's drinking problem. Mostly I wanted Lisette to know that I was proud that she was my wife, and I wanted my father to know the same. "Dad," I said, "this is *ma femme*—my wife—Lisette."

Dad offered his hand well in front of him. Lisette took it and then embraced him. "Monsieur Delafield, I am happy to meet you. I love Fran very much." It was clear from the halting manner in which she spoke that she'd rehearsed her little speech, and then her green eyes overflowed with tears, and she spoke in French. "I will make your son a good wife. I will make you proud that I am your daughter. I did not mean to bring shame to your family, and I pray that you and Madame Delafield will love me someday, too."

I tried to comfort her as my father asked what Lisette had said.

"She said she loves Fran," Heather answered. "That she didn't mean to shame our family. That she hopes someday you and Mom will love her and be proud that she's a member of our family. Frankly, Daddy, I can't see how you can ask for much more than that. Being loved is all anybody ever really wants, Fran and me included. So give her a chance. Philadelphia society and our family may discover something none of us ever knew."

"Only time will tell," our father said. "Only time will tell." We stood in awkward silence waiting for him to continue. His French was formal, spoken slowly but precisely. "I hope you will be happy here."

I looked at Heather, and she at me, as though we couldn't believe what we'd just heard. Lisette thanked him, and he nodded and said, *"Bonne nuit,"* and walked to the stairs and up to his wife and to bed.

"I will make it work, Fran," Lisette said. "I will, no matter how hard it is for them."

At the time I thought if anyone could, it would be Lisette.

Married Life

During the five short days that Lisette and I were together be-fore I went off to Dartmouth—days she happily called our *lune de miel* even though it was a honeymoon like no other I could have imagined—I fell in love with her all over again, and, while at first I'd thought that I'd done the responsible thing, I became convinced that it would all work out, one way or the other, because we loved one another so. But, there was little for us to do that didn't run the risk of being seen by someone who knew me. As a result, we were prisoners in our own home. On top of that, we couldn't seem to find a place, other than my bedroom or by the pool, where our presence wasn't uncomfortable, not only for my parents but for Lisette and me. We always seemed to be in the wrong place at the wrong time, excusing ourselves and moving from the terrace to the living room or out to the pool to keep from being what Mom frequently called "underfoot."

It was during this time that I realized that when Lisette said something, she meant it, perhaps more than anyone I'd ever known. Having said that she was going to make our new life work, she went about it with a vengeance. She began by substituting her formal "Madame" and "Monsieur" with "Mother" and "Father" Delafield and greeted them in English, always adding a short phrase as a result of Heather's and my coaching, asking how they were or if she could do something for them. However, her offers to help weren't met with much enthusiasm. My mother barely tolerated her presence in the kitchen and shooed her away when she offered to weed her small flower garden.

But, I was amazed that none of this seemed to dampen Lisette's optimism, and during the many hours I spent alone with her, she talked of our life once she would no longer be hidden, no longer kept a secret. During one of our talks at the edge of the pool, she put her arm around my waist and spoke softly, as though she didn't want anyone to overhear her. "What would you like to name our baby?"

I hadn't thought that far ahead but said that if it was a boy, maybe I'd just give him my name.

"Not your father's?"

As hurtful and unnerving as it was for me, I said, "Not unless things change, and I doubt they will."

"Perhaps we should wait and see," Lisette said. "We have time, and it could make him so proud."

"Maybe. Maybe not," I said. "And what if it's a girl? Caroline, after your sister?"

"No. Francine." She smiled and kissed me on the cheek. "It is a beautiful name and, one way or another, will tie us together forever."

Surprisingly, that evening after one of the many long periods of silence during dinner, Dad asked if I'd thought about taking Lisette to Willow Grove Park, the local amusement park. "I don't think you'd run into anyone there you know," he said, "and it might be fun."

Heather said she thought it was a brilliant idea, but when I asked if she'd like to join us, she declined, saying that the last time she'd been there, she'd chucked her cookies on the family sitting in front of her on the roller coaster, and she didn't think anyone wanted a repeat of that.

Once at the amusement park, Lisette, was wide eyed with enjoyment. She'd never seen anything like it, and her enthusiasm was contagious. She rode the roller coaster a second time and urged the Ferris wheel operator to stop with us at its top so she could look at the lights of Philadelphia, her new home, in the distance. She tried to win a stuffed panda by throwing a baseball at a series of bowling pins and, when she couldn't do it, said she knew I could.

As we walked through the park, she seemed oblivious to the stares that her beauty attracted. She laughed, and, clutching her large stuffed animal and holding my hand, she frequently kissed me. For a moment we forgot what we were running from and acted as though we didn't have a care in the world. Then suddenly Lisette stopped. "Oh my God, that is Potter, no?"

I looked ahead of us. Lisette was right; there was Potter buying something at the food stand. Not only that, he was buying it for Sidney—Sidney with the bodacious you-know-whats. I turned Lisette away from them, and we half walked, half trotted to the safety of the family Plymouth. Once in the car, Lisette giggled. "My God, that was close! Maybe he did not want to be seen either."

When I didn't seem to see the humor in the situation, Lisette asked why. I stared at the steering wheel and told her how much I hated to have to hide her from one of my best friends and couldn't wait until we were free to live our lives like normal people. She comforted me by saying that it would all work out in time. I prayed that she was right and told her about Potter and Sidney and what had really taken place in La Malbaie, adding that I was surprised to see them together again.

"Ah, Fran," Lisette said, "you are so naïve. Potter would like to bed every girl he sees."

"Potter?" I said.

"Certainly. Potter. I am surprised he did not try to take me away from you."

I said he wouldn't have done that.

"No?" She pushed my shoulder as though I was kidding her. "And why not?"

Maybe she was right, I thought. If Potter hadn't been consumed by his problem with Sidney and could have navigated the language barrier, why not? I offered up, "Because he's my friend."

Lisette kissed me and told me that she would accept my answer, even though she thought it was wishful thinking.

The night before I was to leave for Dartmouth, I asked my parents if they now understood why I loved Lisette so. They looked at one another, expressionless. Mom reached for her old-fashioned but stopped. She looked down at her trembling hands and seemed to struggle with the words that followed. "No matter, Fran. That is irrelevant. Rest assured she will be given proper care."

I was somewhat encouraged by her comment and waited for her to continue or for my father to say something, but he looked away.

I waited a moment more. "That's it?"

"What more should you expect?" my mother said.

"Geez, Mom, I don't know, maybe something like she sure is trying to make this work or...or something like that." I could feel my anger rising and figured what the hell, maybe I'd already waited too long to unload on them. "I've heard all your lectures on right and wrong, on my responsibilities, and on the impact that our irresponsible behavior has had on our family, so now both of you listen to me for a change. Lisette is your daughter-in-law. Got it? My wife. Mrs. Francis Hopkinson Delafield Jr. She didn't mean to shame you, so why can't you give her a chance? Isn't that your responsibility, Mom, and yours, too, Dad? How good is the fine old Delafield name if it represents a family that can't love someone who isn't in the *Social Register*? Can't forgive someone who has made a mistake? A costly mistake, I'll admit, but an innocent, natural mistake? So cut her some slack, and me, too. If you'd just look and listen a little closer and view her with an open mind, you'd see that I couldn't have found a better girl anywhere."

Both Mom and Dad were speechless.

From her bedroom window, Heather yelled down to the terrace, "Atta boy, Franny! Atta boy!"

Dad wagged his finger in Heather's direction and started to say something but stopped. Lisette was standing at the door, tears sliding down her cheeks as though she'd understood every word I'd said. "It is okay, Fran. Please do not be upset with your parents. It is new for me and also for them. They have taken me in, and that is the first step. I will be safe here while you are studying. We all must give this time."

Mom flinched at Lisette's words and turned to Dad. "My God, but she's a clever one."

"What did she say?" he asked.

Again Heather called from her window. "She said everything will be okay in time, but, frankly, Daddy, she's a lot more optimistic than I am. And while you're at it, could you both begin to refer to her as 'Lisette' rather than always calling her 'she' and 'her'? It might help you realize that you're dealing with a real person here, not some inanimate object, for Pete's sake."

After that encounter, nothing more was said about Lisette's and my situation, except the following day, as my father drove me to the North Philadelphia train station, he assured me that Lisette would be taken good care of, that I had nothing to worry about.

Dartmouth and Beyond

When I arrived at Dartmouth, the newsy, pain-in-the-ass brochure that introduced the freshmen described me this way—almost as though I was the only guy from a private school in the freshman class:

> The only graduate of the (oh-so-exclusive!) Episcopal School to grace our campus this year, Fran Delafield hails from an upper-crust Philadelphia suburb and is a shoe-in to make the freshman baseball squad as he led all New England high school pitchers in games won and strikeouts over the last four years. 310 Gile Hall; Gold Coast cluster.

As annoying as it was, I thought the write-up could have been worse; it could have said that I was a married man whose pregnant wife didn't speak English and was hidden like a fugitive in his parents' home some three hundred and fifty miles away.

At first my calls home were filled with reassurances from Lisette that her pregnancy was going well; she had yet to experience any morning sickness, hadn't gained any weight, and wouldn't show for at least another month. When I asked if she thought things were changing with Mom and Dad, she sighed and let out a gentle laugh. "I am trying very hard to make them accept me. As your father often says, only time will tell, only time will tell."

But, after a few weeks, Lisette's tone began to change. In early October she was crying when I called, and my father interrupted us by taking the phone from her. "This situation has become untenable for your mother," he said. "She no longer has any privacy, and Lisette has made little progress with her English. We have no idea what to do with her when we have guests, and we can't really explain who she is or why she's living with us. Frankly, Fran, it's one hell of a mess."

The first thing that came to my mind was, "No shit, Dick Tracy." I was tempted to remind him that having Lisette live with them was their idea, not mine. Neither of us spoke for a long while, as though we were baiting each other to make the next move.

Finally, I took a deep breath and asked Dad what he wanted me to do. "Right now I'm not sure," he said and handed the phone back to Lisette.

"What's going on?" I asked. "Are you all right?"

"No. I am not all right. Your parents do not want me here, and you are far away."

"But, Lisette, if Mom and Dad—"

"It is not only them. I am very lonely without you and have nothing to do." She muffled a sob, and then she startled me. Surprised and worried the hell out of me. "We are too young for all of this. We have made a terrible mistake, my beloved, and are paying our separate prices. Hiding me to avoid the shame makes me feel like an animal in a cage. I need my freedom, to get my life back."

"Please, Lisette, don't talk that way," I pleaded. "Please. It's not me who is hiding you, and it's only until our child is born."

For a moment Lisette didn't respond. Then she asked, "And how will our baby change all this?"

"Because then my parents will have to accept that we are married and have a child. They will be forced to realize that their dream that those truths will somehow go away is nothing more than wishful thinking."

"Perhaps you are right, but that is months away. I do not know if I can live like this until then."

I found it hard to draw a breath, to keep my thoughts in order, and wondered how it had come to this. Wondered what had happened to change our roles, making me the one who was arguing to commit to the future. "Please, give it a little more time. If things don't get better soon, I'll come home and we'll start over. Maybe here in Hanover. Maybe in Canada. We'll find a way. We must."

"I will do as you ask, but I am afraid we will be unhappy no matter what."

"Don't say that. For God's sake, Lisette, don't say that," I said. "I love you, and we will be happy. Please hold on just a little while longer."

I was fighting back tears when I heard her whisper, "I will always love you," and she hung up.

That night I woke up, my heart pounding in a wave of panic, breaths not coming easily. Lisette was right, we—no, I, goddamn it—had made a terrible mistake. What's more, I'd been duped by my parents, and I cursed myself for playing into their hands. Hadn't Heather warned me that it was a game of attrition? And it appeared that they'd won. What's worse, I'd acted like a child, not like a married man, and the distance between Hanover and home was all they needed to keep me out of the equation. It was clear that it wasn't Lisette's pregnancy that was the issue; the issue lay in the solution that my parents had mandated and that I'd stupidly agreed to. And I made up my mind, then and there, to drop out of Dartmouth and start a new and different life with Lisette.

Early the next morning, I called home to tell her of my plan, but the phone rang and rang and rang without answer.

I called that evening during the cocktail hour, and my mother said that my wife was resting. With that one comment, I was even more convinced that going home was the right decision because Mom still wouldn't—or couldn't—call Lisette by name. I said that I didn't care what she was doing, that I needed to talk to her.

"Perhaps tomorrow. I'm afraid she's not feeling well."

"What's wrong?" I asked.

"Having a child takes a toll on a woman's body, even if she is only a teenager. You should have known that before you followed the course you've chosen. But, don't worry, in time she'll be better. Call midweek. I think things will have settled down by then."

I pressed her to tell me what was going on.

"Please, Fran," my mother said. "Bill and Ginny Ames are here for supper, and I'm being rude taking time away from them. Bill still talks about your big fish and—"

I told her that I couldn't care less about all of that, that I was coming home, and asked her to tell Lisette that I'd see her Thursday or Friday at the latest.

"Let's talk on Wednesday, dear," Mom said as though she hadn't heard a word about my plans to come home. "All should be fine by then."

She hung up, leaving me confused and angry, but mostly worried that there were things going on at home that I wasn't aware of, that I couldn't control. Again, I felt that I had been stupid to go off to Hanover while Mom and Dad tried to resolve what they viewed as their dilemma in a fashion acceptable to them.

My worst fears became a reality when I picked up my mail the following afternoon.

My beloved Fran,

By the time you receive this, I will be back in Quebec, where I hope and pray I belong. Since our last conversation I have done nothing but think about us, our love, our child, and our future. I even talked with your mother about it, but she was very hard and determined. As you say, it is their adult logic against our youthful love. They do not understand how deeply we feel about each other, and your mother repeated many times that we were too young to be married and raise a child. She said that I will have a very difficult time fitting into your life no matter what, that not speaking English, even though I promised her that I would learn, and being Catholic and not having gone to the correct American schools would always make me an outsider. She also said that until you finish college our lives will be poor, complicated, and unhappy.

So, my beloved, it is now clear that I didn't understand so many, many things about your life, your family, and the importance of what we had done. I was wrong to force you into this situation, and you are my hero for trying to fulfill my dreams. But you are also a blind prophet who could not see the future as clearly as I prayed you would. And so I have lifted our burden from your family and you. I have time to get our marriage annulled and will do that. And I will take care of our baby so you will never have to worry about that again.

While I am only eighteen, I believe you will be the only man I will ever love. I cannot write any more. The pain is too great. I will love you forever and wish you Godspeed in all that you do. Believe me when I say I am doing this for you so you can start anew.

Your loving wife and friend, forever,
Lisette

I read the letter over and over and thought, how could they? I'd never had a chance to talk her out of this. I wondered what they'd done to get her to agree to leave me. I can save this, I thought, and called home, but there was no answer.

I called an hour later. Still no one answered.

Finally, at seven o'clock, my father picked up the phone, and I exploded. "What the hell did you do, Dad? Why didn't you let me know? You and Mom owe me an explanation about my wife. My future. You went behind my back like we were playing some kind of game."

"Easy, Fran. We didn't do anything," he said. "It was her decision."

"The hell you didn't do anything. She told me about her conversation with Mom. *You* promised me that she'd be taken good care of, Dad, that I had nothing to worry about. *You* let me down, Dad. Worse, you went back on your word."

"Look, Fran, this has been a very difficult time for all of us, especially your mother," my father said. "Lisette finally realized that she'd made a huge mistake and took the five thousand dollars and promised to clean up the whole mess."

"You're kidding," I said. "She wouldn't do that."

"I hate to say it, Son, but I told you all along that she would. In a way you're better off that she left, and in time even you and she may agree. I know it's a bitter pill for the two of you to swallow, but I think it's true. Now you can study and play ball without any distractions." He paused. "And rejoin the Delafield family."

"Not a chance, Dad," I said. "Not a snowball's prayer in hell." And I hung up.

Panicked, I ran to the college bookstore, got a handful of change, and called Lisette from my dorm. Her father answered the phone and told me never to call her again, that his whore daughter would be moving from La Malbaie to hide her shame and she didn't want to hear from me. He added that he didn't want to either, that I was the bastard who created the problem, and hung up.

Next I called René, who said he'd been expecting my call. "I have just received some very, very sad news."

"How is she?" I asked. "Where is she? How do I reach her?"

"You cannot reach her. She asked that I keep her whereabouts a secret."

"Her life a secret from me? She is my wife, René. Remember?"

"Only too well, and I am very sad for you both, but I promised to protect her."

"Protect her from her husband?" I said.

"No, protect her from this nightmare. She needs some distance from all of this, but she asked that I tell you how much she loves you and always will."

"It appears she loved the money more than me."

René made his *pfiff* sound and spoke in English. "Don't be absurd, Francis. You know that's not the case. She needed the money to take care of her child. I will send you the papers for annulment in a few days. You need not come here; simply sign them and return them to me, and I will do the rest." He paused. "I honestly think it's best if you leave Lisette alone. *Vraiment.* The pain on her face is more than I can stand, and I don't know what she will do if you confuse her even further. She is, as you Americans say, at her wits' end. Please be strong and kind, as I know you can."

"But, René, she is everything to me," I said. "Everything, and I don't want to lose her."

"I'm afraid you have, but you are young, and you will heal, maybe not completely, but you will heal from this and move on. That is the way of the human spirit. I am flattered that you called me and will look after Lisette for you. That I promise. Perhaps someday we will fish together again. I'd like that very much."

"Fish together? Fuck off!" I slammed the receiver down and screamed, "Why did they do this to me? Why did *she* do this to me? I quit. I fucking quit!"

One of my roommates rushed to the hall and asked if I was all right. I said not by a long shot and stared at the Dartmouth motto on the note pad that held René's phone number: *Vox Clamantis In Deserto*. How ironic, I thought. I was that voice of one crying in the wilderness and yelled, "Well, I'm out of this fucking wilderness. Hanover and my family and the whole fucking world can kiss my ass good-bye."

Sûreté du Québec

I drove a borrowed car all night, mostly in an unrelenting downpour, stopping only for gas and coffee, and was jumpy from caffeine and the uppers one of my roommates had given me to keep me awake. Perhaps it was the rainy, gray October weather and the pall it cast on everything, but when I arrived in La Malbaie the next day, the street Lisette lived on looked more run down and smaller than it had during my visits in the summer. What's more, her garage was empty, and I didn't know if that meant she wasn't home or her father wasn't home or both. As I got out of the car and began to stretch and work the kinks out of my neck, I heard a man's voice say, "Francis Delafield?"

A policeman stood across the street from Lisette's house, leaning against a cruiser marked *Sûreté du Québec*. He was tall, kind of gangling, with a long, thick neck. Even on this gray morning, he wore dark aviator's glasses. He slapped a clipboard against his thigh, and he walked toward me and said my name again. I thought for sure that Lisette's father had called the cops and that the man planned to arrest me, though for what, I had no idea.

I said I was Francis Delafield, and the policeman asked if I spoke French. When I told him that I did, he said, "I've heard so," and smiled and told me to relax and opened the passenger door to his cruiser and signaled for me to get in.

Once seated in the car, the officer placed the clipboard on his lap and ran his finger down a series of handwritten notes. "Monsieur Delafield, I am here to help you, not apprehend you. We received a call last night from Monsieur Trudeau's assistant, René Jaud, who told us of your situation and asked us to watch it closely. Given Monsieur Trudeau's position in the community, we took this call very seriously." Still wearing his dark glasses, he turned toward me. "I'm sure you understand."

I nodded but wondered what was coming next.

"A couple of things have happened since Monsieur Jaud called. He thought his brother represented a threat to his niece, and we agreed. Last night we arrested him for being drunk, disorderly, and disturbing the peace. Eventually we added resisting arrest to his charges. In addition, we received a call this morning from the diner where you had breakfast alerting us that you were here in La Malbaie. And, following Monsieur Jaud's recommendation, we've elected to intervene. We are confident that Monsieur Trudeau would approve."

I was both amused and pissed off by the cop's formal French and his fatherly approach toward me, considering that he couldn't have been much older than I was—certainly no more than twenty-five. "So, your friend is safe for now and is in the custody of her uncle," he said. "You have nothing to worry about."

Nothing to worry about? That was Dad's promise, too. "Listen," I said, "she's not just a friend, she's my wife, for God's sake, so skip all that custody bullshit. I must have the right to see my wife."

"I'm afraid that is impossible." He glanced at the notes on his clipboard. "Monsieur Jaud has asked me to assure you that your wife is in the best of hands and that, as he apparently told you on the telephone, this course of action is best for all concerned." He waited for me to say something, but I had no idea what to say or do next.

Finally, the officer said, "Monsieur Jaud asked me to tell you that he can't be reached by phone. He also asked me to wish you well in college."

"That's it? Good luck in college? Come on, officer, is there no way I can see Lisette?"

"No. There is no way."

I told him again that I didn't understand how he, or anyone else for that matter, could legally stop me from seeing my wife.

The policeman hesitated, then flipped through the papers on his clipboard. "An emergency protective order has been prepared. All hope it won't be necessary to implement it."

"A what?" I asked. "What are you talking about?"

The officer set the clipboard in a holder between the seats and turned toward me. "It is very simple, very direct and enforceable. The order prevents you from…" He paused and took off his dark glasses and set them on the dash. "From seeing your wife. Believe me, I know how hard this is for you."

"You do, do you?" I said. "You've got to be kidding. How in hell could you have any idea what I'm feeling?"

The policeman looked away and ran a hand over the steering wheel. "My wife has left me, too. We've been married less than a year and, like you, there's nothing I can do. So I know how frustrating and infuriating it can be."

I told him that I was sorry and hoped it would all work out. The officer thanked me but said he doubted that it would, that there was another man involved. He shook his head. *C'est la vie.*

I, too, muttered, *"C'est la vie,"* and thought both of us were too young to be having this conversation. "Are you sure there's nothing that can be done?"

The policeman chuckled. "For you or for me?"

"Either or both."

"I'm afraid not," he said, and we sat in silence. After a moment, he reached to shake my hand. "Good luck at…It is Dartmouth, no?"

I was surprised that he knew about Dartmouth, and I wondered how much René had told him about Lisette and me. "You know of Dartmouth?"

"Certainly." He smiled. "I graduated from McGill last year and played hockey against Dartmouth several times. You were good, but not as good as us." The smile left his face as quickly as it had appeared. "I went into law enforcement to support us while I was waiting to go to law school. Now, without my wife, I do not know if I will go through with my plans. The tuition is very expensive."

I couldn't believe that I was sitting in a cop car in a tiny town in Quebec with a total stranger talking to him the way I would with an old friend about our marriages and college athletics, wondering aloud how we were going to make our dreams, shattered as they were, come true.

We shook hands and for a moment studied each other. "Good luck, Francis," the policeman said. "Maybe it will all work out for you someday."

I thanked him and said, "Good luck to you, too, officer."

"It's Bernard."

"Well, Bernard, maybe it will work out for you, too. All we can do is hope."

"Yes," Bernard said, "all we can do is hope."

Bernard waited for me to drive away. I guess he also waited to see if I would return. But I didn't go back. Instead I drove to M. Trudeau's to see if I could find René, but there was a chain across the drive, and all the buildings were locked and the main house shuttered for the winter. I was walking around the property for old time's sake when a wave of remorse and nostalgia swept over me, and—for one last time—I peered in the window of the cabin where Lisette and I had first professed our love. The small couch was covered with clear plastic, the table cleared of its magazines, and the bedroom door was closed. Not at all the way we had left it.

I trudged back to the car and crawled into the backseat to get some sleep before beginning the long drive back to Hanover. As I lay curled in a ball, hands jammed between my knees for warmth, I realized that without a doubt everything was stacked against Lisette and me: circumstance, my family, and now, the law. After a few moments, I gave up trying to sleep and drove south, wondering if Bernard would ever be reunited with his wife, and if I'd ever see Lisette again.

Earning My Keep

When I'd headed off to Dartmouth, my father had pressed me to "earn my keep" by sending one hundred dollars home every month to pay for Lisette's room and board. But the minute Lisette took Dad's $5,000 and fled to Canada, Dad upped the ante and sent me a note saying that he expected me to reimburse him. As he put it, "To pay for my costly mistakes." At the time I wondered if Dad was being pressured by Mom, or if D3—his architecture firm of Draper, Dixon & Delafield—was in financial trouble. Maybe both. But I knew that Dad would never admit either to me.

And so, once back in Hanover, I was trying to figure out how I was going to meet Dad's new financial demand when I got a phone call from Potter. He was drunk and alternated between hysterical laughter and choking, whining sobs. He started off by asking, "How they hanging?" but before I could think of some witty retort, he told me that he'd just been suspended from Princeton for calling some professor a faggot and punching his lights out. I tried to slow him down, but he talked on, saying over and over that he'd screwed up big time, that his old man was furious and had every right to be.

When he finally stopped to take a breath, I asked him what he was going to do. Potter quickly answered that he was going to join the paratroopers. "What the hell, Delafield, it should be a ball." He laughed. "Only three of them were killed last week on a jump at Fort Campbell. Want to come along?"

As surprised as I was by Potter's invitation, I was even more surprised by my positive reaction and found myself saying that I'd think about it. Seriously give it some thought. Potter rambled on for a while more. When he'd run out of gas, he muttered something about the two of us being war heroes just like our fathers and hung up.

The more I thought about it, the more convinced I became that Potter's idea wasn't harebrained after all; his drunken ranting may have provided me with an answer to my financial dilemma and to a lot of other things as well. I thought it would be a good way for me to make enough money to pay Dad back while meeting my service obligation at the same time, because in 1955 unless you were 4-F or married, sooner or later you got drafted. And there were few ifs, ands, or buts about it. Moreover, I thought joining the army would put some distance between me and the mess that I found myself in.

While most of our friends would eventually sign up for ROTC or go to the navy officer candidate school after graduating from college, Potter and I came up with our own scheme: we would enlist in the paratroopers after the first of the year so that I could complete my semester at Dartmouth. Unlike Potter, however, I wouldn't say anything to my parents until shortly before Potter and I were to leave for the army. It was a well-thought-out plan, a responsible plan, maybe even a plan that my parents would have a hard time faulting.

⸺ ∞ ⸺

I bummed a ride home for Thanksgiving only to have to put up with my parents behaving as though the situation with Lisette had never taken place. I counted the hours until Friday morning when Potter would pick me up to drive us to the enlistment center. I was laughing with relief and a smug sense of satisfaction as I got in his car and told him that my parents were going to shit their pants when they found out what I was up to.

Potter didn't smile, didn't seem to see the humor in the situation. He just stared at his hands, which he held together at the top of the steering wheel. Finally he said, "Delafield, I'm sorry. Really sorry." He paused for quite a while; then he went on to say that the night before he'd had a long talk with his father, who'd convinced him that three years were too long to be away from Princeton and that he should join the City Troop for six months.

I was stunned by Potter's change in plans, even though I thought that joining the City Troop, the local National Guard unit, would have been what my parents would want for me, too. The First Troop Philadelphia City Cavalry was the country's oldest active military unit and, as such, was old-guard Philadelphia, its blue-blood, historic roll call including many of my ancestors as well as Potter's. The perfect option for a Morris or a Delafield.

Once again, Potter's bombshell reminded me that he was still very much under his father's influence because this decision, and many of his others, was his father's doing. I wondered when, and if, that would change.

When I asked if I could borrow his car, he looked puzzled. "You're going without me?"

I realized that this might be the first time I could remember that I wasn't relying on Potter in a critical situation. I mustered my courage and decided to say to hell with him. I'd followed his lead too many times. Leaving La Malbaie without checking with M. Trudeau and pitching to Fairburn in the Andover game, to name but two. No, I'd make up my own mind no matter what Potter or my parents wanted. None of them were going to change my plans, and I tried to convince myself that it was okay.

When I said yes, I was going without him, Potter said, "Really? What about Dartmouth? Why not join the Troop with me?"

I drew a deep breath and made sure that he was looking at me to make the point that I was dead serious. "Fuck Dartmouth," I said. "And fuck the City Troop. You don't know the half of what's going on with me. I've got to do this. I've got to get out on my own and get away from all this family bullshit for a while."

The recruiting sergeant at 401 North Broad Street gave me my first glimpse of how the army worked. When I signed in as Francis H. Delafield Jr., the sergeant asked if my father was Francis H. Delafield Sr. The conversation that followed reminded me of an Abbott and Costello routine:

"No, sir. My father's Theodore Delafield. I was named after my grandfather."

"So your grandfather's senior?" the sergeant asked.

"He was, sir."

"You mean he's dead?"

"Yes, sir. He died last year."

"Then you're senior. Once a senior dies, the junior moves up."

"I understand, sir, but my father said it was too much of a hassle to change all my records after my grandfather died."

"Max nix to me," the sergeant said, and I fulfilled my military obligation as Francis H. Delafield *Senior*.

The IQ test and the physical took place without incident. When the doctor was through examining me, he closed his folder and pushed it to one side of his desk. "You're in great shape," he said. "Healthy as a horse. But do you mind if I ask you a question?" It was obvious he wasn't looking for an answer and went on to say, "You're a smart kid, Francis, so what are you doing joining the paratroops? Why not flight school or military intelligence? Something a little more...more sensible."

I didn't have a good answer, and I told him so. I said that it's what I'd decided to do and that I'd experienced one too many changes recently to make another. The doctor stood and shook my hand. "Well, son, it's your ass, not mine. Good luck running around with all those crazies."

When he turned me back to the recruiting sergeant, the sergeant's first question was when would I be ready to go. I started to say sometime after I'd completed my semester at college, but, seeing that I already owed Dad $5,000 and that, with my scholarship, he'd paid Dartmouth far less than full tuition, I wondered what difference adding another $100 to $200 would make. What the hell, I thought, the sooner I got started earning money and getting away from my parents the better, and I told the sergeant that I was ready to go as soon as the army would take me.

My parents were horrified, saying that this was nothing more than another impetuous decision on my part. They argued, over and over, that the least I could have done was complete the semester they'd paid for and then quietly taken a leave of absence. And, of course, they asked if I'd considered the City Troop.

Obviously they didn't understand that I was mad as hell at them—and, it seemed, at the whole world—and wanted to escape from them and all the established expectations and go somewhere where no one knew or cared who I was as soon as I could. While I knew that, to their way of thinking, they were right, I tried to explain that I'd decided to stop acting like a lemming and take charge of my life for a change, that I would pay them everything I owed them, including the first semester's tuition. What more could they ask?

"You're in the Army Now"

Thursday, December 1, 1955, I enlisted in the army.

Dad drove me to the recruiting office but only spoke once, to ask if I was sure I was doing the right thing. When I said, "Yes, sir," he said that we should have talked more about it, and about lots of other things, and turned on the radio, saying that he wanted to get the traffic report.

When we said our good-byes, Dad pressed his St. Christopher's medal in the palm of my hand. "It got me through the Bulge," he said, "without a scratch. I hope it'll bring you luck, too."

I asked him if he was sure he wanted me to have the medal because I knew how much he treasured it. "Absolutely sure," he said. "The goal here is to get you back in one piece."

I had taken a few steps toward the recruiting office when I heard him call my name. He'd lit a cigarette and was leaning through the car window, beckoning for me to come back. "One piece of military advice?" He was smiling. "Just remember, Fran: fuck them fucking fuckers."

Stunned, I held all my personal belongings in a small gym bag in one hand and my father's St. Christopher's in the other as I watched him ease the family Plymouth slowly into the rush-hour traffic on

Broad Street. I finally realized that Dad understood the world I was about to enter better than most, that his military experience hadn't been limited to his impressive uniform or his Third Army Zippo, and I wanted him to stop so we could talk about what he'd been through and what I was about to go through. But it was too late. And it was, I thought, one hell of a way to leave home. To join the army.

On the train ride to South Carolina, I stared out the window as I sped farther and farther from home and thought back on my father's parting words. The swearing had surprised me—a lot actually—but his swearing wasn't the main issue. The issue was how out of character it was for him to talk with me as a friend when he disapproved so of what I was doing. That's what really confused me. On the other hand, it was typical of Dad, always leaving me to work things through on my own. Making me do the work.

Then, as if I needed another reminder that I was entering a world foreign to me, when the train arrived in Columbia, before I boarded the army bus to Fort. Jackson, I hurried to the restroom where an elderly Negro man held up his hand and said, as though he didn't want anyone else to hear him, "Yours is next door." I could tell the man sensed that I had no idea what he was talking about, and he pointed to the COLORED sign above the men's room door. I thanked him, and he smiled and shook his head and walked away, as though he'd had this experience many times before.

My first month at Fort Jackson wasn't at all what I'd expected. The training cycle for me and the other recruits who dribbled in up until a few days before Christmas wasn't scheduled to start until early January. Consequently, we new recruits spent all of our time at the mercy of a veteran of the Korean conflict and our platoon sergeant, Sergeant First Class Kirchner.

Under Sergeant Kirchner's careful watch, we were taken for longer and longer runs twice a day to get us ready for basic training.

And, after the runs, we participated in what became known as "Operation Chickenshit": cleaning the barracks, practicing how to make up our bunks, polishing our boots and shoes, disassembling and assembling the M1 rifle, and then cleaning the barracks and making up our bunks and polishing our footwear and taking down our weapons once again.

During our free time—and there was more than enough of it—we lounged in the dayroom in front of a large black-and-white TV set, our heroes being chain-smoking Sgt. Joe Friday on *Dragnet*, and "the one, the only" Groucho Marx on *You Bet Your Life*. Sunday mornings we watched Oral Roberts on *The Abundant Life*, making fun of his promise to heal his viewers if they'd put their hands on their sets. (This promise was almost always followed by Carlos Ramirez, a Puerto Rican draftee, jumping from his chair and clutching the TV, pleading for Roberts to heal his aching *huevos*.)

On Christmas Day I called home and talked briefly with Mom and Dad before they handed me over to Heather. When she asked how I was doing and I said that I was fine, Heather said I was going to get coal in my stocking if I kept up that charade. While she never failed to make me laugh, when I hung up, the sorrow of losing Lisette and the loneliness of my situation washed over me, and I decided not to call home the following week to wish everyone a happy new year. It certainly didn't look like it was going to be a happy one for me, and I sensed that my parents wouldn't miss my call.

Beginning in the second week in January, basic training began in earnest, and, mercifully, I no longer had time to worry about the mess I'd created or to feel sorry for myself. My fate was no longer in my hands; I was nothing more than Private Delafield at the beck and call of Sergeant Kirchner, a man who knew nothing of my history and, if he had, would have said he couldn't have cared less. Things were just the way I wanted them.

The brightest moment during the two months of basic training came barely a week after it had begun. At mail call on January 17ᵗʰ I was handed two envelopes by Sergeant Kirchner, who said, "Nineteen or twenty, Delafield?"

I was caught off guard by his question but then pulled myself to attention. "Nineteen, Sergeant."

"Let me guess," he said. "Cards from your girlfriend and your folks."

I lowered my voice. "No, Sergeant. My sister and my father's secretary."

He looked me up and down and shook his head. "That's a new one on me. Well, celebrate by getting a haircut. Or a flea collar. Take your pick."

Dutifully I bellowed, "Yes, Sergeant!" As I pivoted to rejoin my platoon, I heard Sergeant Kirchner say, almost in a whisper, "Happy birthday, son."

I found the cards heartening, like someone actually cared about me. Heather's was filled with love and support. The card from Anita, Dad's former secretary who over the years had displayed an uncanny knack for having celebratory cards for Heather and me arrive on the exact date of the event, included this type-written note:

```
Dear Fran:
    I hope things are going well for you at Fort
Jackson. To cheer you, your enlisting made me
think of a song we used to sing during our war:
    "You're in the Army now  You're not behind a
plow  You'll never get rich  You son of a bitch
You're in the Army now." I think the real words
were "digging a ditch," but no one ever sang it
that way. No matter, it makes me smile and brings
back so many, many memories, both happy and sad.
    Have a fun, safe birthday.
```

```
And praise the Lord and pass the ammunition.
(Sorry, I couldn't resist!)
Fondly,
Anita
```

Anita's note took me back to the letters Dad had written me while I was at Episcopal. They were short and, for lack of a better word, bland. It was as though the distance between Chestnut Hill and New Hampshire had drawn a curtain between us, for even though I wrote chatty letters home every week about my grades and sports and goings-on at school, I rarely heard from Dad, and when I did, he never addressed the things that I'd written about to him. (Now that I've looked back on his letters, they all have *td/ao'l* typed at the bottom, indicating that Dad had dictated them to Anita, making me wonder if he seemed so removed and businesslike because Anita was listening in.)

After completing my infantry training at Fort Jackson, I was transferred to the 82nd Airborne at Fort Bragg, where I turned even more inward and did nothing more than try to be a really good soldier and write Lisette, pleading with her to answer me, to let me know how she was doing, to forgive my parents and let me back into her life. My letters were never returned, and I assumed that Lisette had received them but chose not to answer. That was as confusing, frustrating, and hurtful as anything I'd ever experienced.

Unlike my lengthy letters to Lisette, my letters home weren't much more than short notes to which I attached a check that was augmented by an additional fifty-five dollars a month hazardous-duty pay for jumping out of airplanes, the checks that would in time settle my debt with my father. At least financially.

Say Good-Bye to the 1950's

Ninety-Day Wonder

1958. On a chilly, cloudless afternoon in January, I started my third full year in the army by reporting to the Infantry Officers' Candidate School at Fort Benning. It was there that, along with 220 other enlisted men, I struggled to adjust to close-order harassment by the school's cadre for most of the twenty-two-week course. We were taught the army's concept of a "square meal" (sitting erect on six inches of our chairs, staring straight ahead, moving our forks or spoons in a robot-like fashion straight up to our mouths and then straight down to our food); we ran everywhere, whether it was to formation or class or the barber for the weekly shaving of our heads; and we were driven to survive on four hours of sleep a night with most of us losing more than 10 percent of our body weight in the bargain.

A few weeks after I began my officer's training, a telegram from Anita arrived (as always, precisely on my birthday) wishing me a happy twenty-first and luck as a "ninety-day wonder," the term that Dad often used when referring to lieutenants who had completed OCS during World War II.

Five months later I received my commission, instantly becoming an officer and a gentleman by an act of Congress. I stayed on at Fort Benning to complete the Ranger School before receiving my first posting, my orders assigning me to the 77th Special Forces Group back at Fort Bragg. That assignment marked a period of exhilaration and independence for me because I was earning more than $330 a month and had already settled a large portion of my debt with Dad. That was a tremendously satisfying, liberating feeling, and on at least one occasion, I considered making the army a career, as it seemed a good fit for me and would keep me far away from the life I'd so readily abandoned.

1959. Late spring, within days of Ho Chi Minh's declaration of his "people's war" on South Vietnam, I received orders to ship out to Nha Trang, a training facility about two hundred miles northeast of Saigon, where I was to lead a team of advisers to the Army of the Republic of Vietnam (ARVN). I was delighted with the thought of going to Vietnam because I thought an overseas tour would be exciting, maybe even glamorous, and might give me a new lease on life, something that I had grown to want very badly.

With my orders in hand, I called home, dialing my parents at six forty-five to catch them early in their cocktail hour. My mother answered, and, after a few pleasantries that felt to me like she was distracted by something, I asked that Dad join the call, for I had some important news for them both. Immediately Mom asked, "Are you in trouble?" I assured her that all was well, and then I heard Dad pick up the other phone and greet me as "Son," a term that in the past he'd reserved for the most loving of our conversations, and I felt my throat tighten.

I began by telling them that I was being sent to Vietnam in a few weeks and that I'd be stationed there for thirteen months. "Isn't that an unlucky number?" my mother asked. "And isn't that where we failed so badly at Dien Bien Phu?"

"Gay, I think you're mistaken," my father said. "I don't think we have—"

"*Non, non, non, Theo. Le Français,*" Mom interrupted. "I believe they lost one hundred thousand men there, maybe even more, before they saw the error of their ways."

I tried to ignore Mom's comment about thirteen being an unlucky number and said, yes, it was where the French had failed. She muttered something about men never learning from their mistakes and asked what I was going to do there. Then, before I could answer, she suggested that I explain it to my father, that he understood the military and the way the generals think, or don't think.

When I heard her hang up, I said, "Dad?"

"I'm still here," my father said. He cleared his throat and asked, "Do we have troops there, or are you the first?"

I said we weren't the first, that there were close to nine hundred there already, all part of the president's Military Assistance Advisory Group.

"This was Ike's idea?" my father asked.

General Eisenhower had been Dad's supreme commander at the end of the war, and he viewed him as a really good man, and as a good, solid Republican president. When I told him that it was Ike's idea, he said, "Well, then, it's okay. More than okay." Again he paused. "But here's a kind of funny question: Who are we mad at over there?"

I felt as though I was briefing a superior officer and found myself sliding my heels together, coming to attention. I said we were supporting the South Vietnamese against communist-led guerillas and that the president was turning up the heat by supplying more aid and more advisers. I hurried to ease his anxiety by emphasizing that I'd be an adviser, not a combatant.

Dad said that my mother would be relieved, and asked who else would be going with me.

"Some other shavetails—"

Dad laughed. "God, but I haven't heard that expression in years."

"So it'll be a few of us and some medics and other specialists."

"Interesting," he said and asked if I'd be coming home before I shipped out.

I said I wasn't sure, that I had a lot to do and not much time to do it. The moment I said that, I wished I hadn't. It was a knee-jerk reaction to all that had happened in the past, and I wondered if that wouldn't have been a good time to make amends.

My father sighed. "I understand, but keep in touch, okay? Your mother will worry every day that you're gone."

I thought what my father really meant was that *he* would worry, too, but for some reason he couldn't tell me that. I promised to call before I left and to write more frequently and signed off to Dad's parting words: "Be safe, Son, and come home in one piece."

In one final, desperate letter, I told Lisette where I would be for the next year or so, that I thought of her every day, and hoped that when I came home we could finally be reunited. Once again I had to assume that she received my letter but chose to ignore it, because it was never returned.

Nha Trang

I arrived at Nha Trang Air Base on the coast of Vietnam with two dozen other advisers from Fort Bragg and a handful of instructors from the army language school at the Presidio of Monterey. As we deplaned the C-130 that had shuttled us from Okinawa to Tan Son Nhut Air Base in Saigon and then on to Nha Trang, we hit a wall of humid, ninety-degree weather, only slightly tempered by an occasional breeze from the South China Sea.

I was greeted by Specialist Nogowski. After saluting, he reached to shake my hand and said in a heavy Brooklyn accent that he was the 77th Special Forces' welcoming committee—kind of a Polish Sally Starr, as he put it—and my radio operator. As he threw my duffel bag in the back of his jeep, he added that everybody called him "Nogo" for short and signaled for me to get in. "Okay, Lieutenant, first stop you're to report to the old man. Next I'll get you settled in the honeymoon suite." He laughed and forced the jeep into gear. "Just don't get your hopes up."

I asked if he was referring to my hopes about my new company commander or about my quarters.

"The BOQ," Nogo said. "They're kind of sparse, but the hooch girls keep them clean, so on a scale of one to ten…" He shrugged. "Seven? Seven point five?"

"Sounds good to me. And the CO?"

"Captain Frye? Bleeds olive drab, but he's fair and square. But be advised, Lieutenant, he's colored. Some guys have a problem with that."

I said it wasn't an issue for me.

"Roger that," Nogo said. "His father served with the Triple Nickles in World War II. I think you'll like him." He gave me a quick look with a smile. "Be advised of one other thing, sir: there's a lot less spit-and-polish chickenshit here than there was at Bragg. You remember that, and you'll do just fine. Just fine."

The Nha Trang Air Base had three memorable qualities: lots of palm trees; vast, flat expanses of sand; and row upon row of white clapboard buildings with corrugated metal roofs. With the exception of the black "XVIII Airborne Corps" stenciled above its entrance, the headquarters building was indistinguishable from all the rest. The minute I stepped into Captain Frye's office, I knew what Nogo had meant when he said that the captain bled olive drab. An American flag with gold tassels hung on a pole in one corner and moved slightly as the floor fan's breeze moved across it. Two large photographs, one of President Eisenhower, the other of William Brucker, the secretary of the army, provided the only color to the wall behind him. Seated behind a large gunmetal-gray desk with papers and files neatly stacked in boxes on either side labeled "in" and "out," the captain gave the impression that he had read and signed everything that needed attending to and was in complete control. Unlike Nogo's sweat-stained, wrinkled fatigues, the sleeves of Captain Frye's shirt were sharply creased and rolled neatly above his elbows, his senior parachutist insignia showing snow white above his left breast pocket. When he looked up, I slapped my service cap against my thigh, came to attention, and saluted. "Lieutenant Delafield reporting for duty, sir."

The captain stood and took a long look at me. There was a hint of a smile on his face as though he enjoyed watching me rigidly hold my salute, my eyes fixed straight ahead. I wondered if Nogo would take back his comment about there being less chickenshit at Nha Trang if he could have seen me at that moment. After Captain Frye returned my salute, he reached for my hand and welcomed me, saying that it was nice to have me on board. His tone was warmer, more informal than I had guessed it would be.

He pointed to one of the two chairs in front of his desk, sat, and began to swivel his chair from side to side. He put his large hands to his lips as though he was in prayer and looked at me. He smiled and slid a folder where he could read it, tapped it with the heavy West Point class ring he wore on the ring finger of his left hand, but left the folder unopened. "Your 201 file says two tours at Bragg, plus OCS and Ranger school. But you're barely twenty-two." He paused. "What happened to college?"

I told him that I'd dropped out and left it at that.

He asked from where.

I told him Dartmouth.

He raised his eyebrows. "Oh? An Ivy Leaguer?" He chuckled and asked where I'd gone to high school.

Because of the amused and judgmental manner in which he said "an Ivy Leaguer," I tried to brush his question aside and said that I'd gone to school in New Hampshire. And again, I left it at that.

"High school or prep school?" Before I could answer, the captain said, "Prep school. Right?"

I admitted that he was right.

"Exeter?"

I wondered how he would know about New England boarding schools and shook my head no.

"The Episcopal School?"

I felt my face redden. While he didn't say "the Episcopal School" with the disdain that Skip Fairburn had shown when he called Potter and me "Episcopal pussies" in the Andover game, I thought the captain's tone hinted at the school's elite reputation, and it put me on alert. I had no idea where this conversation was headed, or why it mattered where I went to school. Here I was, having volunteered to serve with one of the army's elite units some nine thousand miles from home, so what difference did it make if I went to Episcopal or Springfield High or Simon Gratz? "For what it's worth, sir," I forced out, "I did graduate from Episcopal."

Captain Frye pulled back in his chair as though he was surprised by the forceful tone of my answer. "No sweat, Lieutenant. I did a PG year at Choate after I graduated from high school in Hawaii. And then—of course—I went to the Point." He twisted his West Point ring and smiled. "This military stuff kind of runs in the family." He waited for me to say something, but I didn't know what more to say. Finally, he said, "We're cool. I've got a feeling we'll do fine together."

He sounded just like Nogo, or had Nogo sounded just like him? Or was that what you said in the army? Well, I was being welcomed as warmly as Captain Frye knew how and told myself not to sweat it, that it was early days. "A question, sir?" I said.

"Fire away."

"Nogo told me that your father was in the army, but I've never heard of the outfit."

"The Triple Nickels?" Captain Frye laughed. "That was the nickname for the 555th, the first negro paratrooper battalion before the army was integrated. They were smoke jumpers and fought a ton of forest fires in the Pacific Northwest at the end of the war. Eventually they became part of the 505 at Fort Bragg." He rolled his ring again. "They're the reason I went to the Point."

"Good for your dad," I said, and found myself sounding older than my years. "He must be very proud of you."

"And me of him. What about your father?"

"Fought in the Bulge with Patton and the Third Army. Ended up a light colonel before returning to civilian life. He's an architect."

The captain was sure my father was proud of me and asked how he felt about me being in Vietnam.

I said that I'd describe his feelings as "mixed." I didn't want to have to explain that Dad's feelings were as mixed about me as they were about me being in Vietnam. Nor did I want to tell the captain how lucky he was to share a mutual respect with his father. The differences in our backgrounds were literally like night and day, and yet I instinctively trusted this man and wanted to prove that I was worthy of his respect.

The captain interrupted my thoughts by saying, "Before Nogo gets you settled in your hooch, let me tell you about your team and who you'll be working with." Without referring to any of his files, he proceeded to give me a thorough description that included the individual strengths and weaknesses of my medic, my automatic weapons expert, my demolition specialist, and Nogo. He concluded by saying that they made up one of the best teams in his command and that I was damn lucky to be their leader.

He was a bit more reserved when it came to Captain Ba, the commanding officer of the ARVN company that I was assigned to. "I'll let you be the judge. Ba means well, and he's good and smart." He paused. "But I suspect that he's not strong enough to do what's right when the shit hits the fan. Military politics are as rampant here as they are back in the States."

Captain Frye was right about the competence of my team. We devoted most of our time to supporting Captain Ba and his men, and, while all was done through interpreters, the ARVN troops seemed to respond well to our drilling them on the basics of small-unit tactics. When not in the field, we supervised their weapons training and spent long hours reinforcing the skills of their radio operators, forward observers, medics, and demolition specialists. Focusing on teaching and training was a welcome break from the routine at Fort Bragg. What's more, it put plenty of distance between my family and me and all our emotional baggage.

Weekends were the highlights of being in country, not only for me but for the other American officers from the air base. When we weren't lounging on the beaches at Nha Trang or Bamboo Island, we treated ourselves to excursions to Saigon, where we made a beeline to the old French colonial hotel, the Continental. I'd first learned about the "Paris of the East" and the Continental during my fifth-form year when we were reading Graham Green's *The Quiet American* but was surprised when I first arrived in Vietnam that the hotel was still flying the French flag. No matter; with a balcony for each room—many of which overlooked the historic opera house—and its flowering frangipani trees and sweet Vietnamese coffee, the Continental reeked of class and history, and we visited it so frequently that we dubbed it the Saigon BOQ, a nickname that clearly didn't do the hotel justice.

Many evenings were devoted to cruising the Saigon River in small boats watching the sun set on the city, or sitting in Sam Lon Square sipping Bière 33 and trying to pick up the ever-flirtatious Vietnamese girls while staring in wonder at the number of mopeds—and the number of people they carried—that wove perilously close to the white-clad traffic cops and in and out of the unnerving traffic without incident.

It should be obvious that my time in the Nam was good. Carefree and very, very good. That is, until I was briefed on my first potential contact with the Viet Cong and, as Nogo put it, "The game changed in a New York minute." Life suddenly become real and earnest, and for the first time I realized that I was becoming embroiled in more than a civil war carried out with pitchforks and ax handles, as it had once been described to me.

Not What I'd Volunteered For

Considering how many men we've lost in Vietnam as I write this in 1968—especially considering what took place earlier this year during the Tet Offensive—recounting my story makes me feel more like a war correspondent than a combatant because what happened to me in 1959 was a freak incident, although it may have been a foreshadowing of the future. And while it has little to do with my family's secrets and struggles, once again Heather has scolded me for sweeping things under the rug and, in this case, keeping some important things bottled up. So, while I know that many of my colleagues view their Vietnam experiences as "sacred stuff," respectfully I'll include this as an important chapter of my life; I'll include it as one of the parts of my story that is most difficult to tell.

The meeting that I assumed was a routine briefing of our joint forces was held in the ARVN's regimental command center. Captain Ba sat with me while Major Thinh spoke haltingly to the officers huddled together. The operation that the major described involved the ARVN's Twelfth Infantry Regiment, which was under his command. As I waited for the interpreter to translate the plan for the few Americans present, Major Thinh nervously circled and tapped his pointer on a large topographical map. His objective was to trap and destroy a dozen or so Viet Cong who had installed a radio transmitter in an area that was nothing more than a checkerboard of rice paddies and dense tree lines a little north of My Lai.

The major wanted Delta Company to set up to the northeast well before daylight while Captain Ba's company, accompanied by me and my team, moved up from the south. Our approach was designed to force the VC to flee to the open fields to the north and east, where they would be engaged by small-arms fire from Delta Company and artillery from the Seventh Division battery. Thinh relied heavily on the fact that his forces overwhelmingly outnumbered the guerillas, and continued to talk about his high level of confidence in a swift, decisive victory.

When Captain Frye asked who I wanted to take, I chose to leave my demolition and automatic weapons experts behind and notified Nogo and my medic, Specialist Henderson, what I had in store for them.

Even though I kept telling myself that up until then no Americans had been killed or wounded in any of these skirmishes, the realization that I wasn't immortal began to interrupt my thoughts, as did the old bromide that there was a first time for everything. And so, with regrets for not going home to say good-bye to my parents, that night I wrote them a letter, along with one to Lisette, and folded both neatly and taped them inside my helmet. Just before turning in, I buttoned Dad's St. Christopher's medal in the left breast pocket of my fatigue shirt and, for the first time since I'd graduated from Episcopal, knelt by my bed and said my prayers, thinking that if there ever was a time to do it, that was it.

On Wednesday, July 8, daylight emerged slowly, shrouded by low cloud cover and torrential rains. Thunder rolled in the west, the shards of lightning that followed brightening the gloom well above the horizon. Nonetheless, well before first light, Bravo Company began to close on the enemy position, trudging directly into wind-driven sheets of rain that reduced visibility and made hearing commands difficult, if not impossible. As I slogged through the mud between Sang, my interpreter—a wiry, sandy-haired mixture of Vietnamese and French ancestry—and Nogo, I heard our call signal crackle over the radio.

"It's Sneaky Pete Five," Nogo said and acknowledged the caller.

The voice on the radio said, "Foxtrot Oscar and Bravo Company are to stay put until further orders. Intel now puts Victor Charlie at more than one hundred. Possibly two hundred. Do you read me?"

"Roger. Five by five," Nogo answered and yelled in my ear, "We're to hold up, sir. There may be as many as two hundred gooks up ahead."

I signaled to Captain Ba to join me and took my interpreter by his sleeve and pulled him close to me. This was our first mission together, and I wanted to make it clear to Sang that he played an important role on our team. I ordered him to tell Captain Ba that we were to hold up, that we were heading into more VC than anticipated.

"Hold up?" Sang said.

"Yes. Hold up," I said in French.

"I understand 'hold up,' Lieutenant, in four different languages," Sang said with a sly smile. "But you must understand, the *di wee* will never agree."

With that unexpected pushback and the scuttle I'd heard that some of the interpreters and journalists in Saigon acted as spies for the VC, suddenly I wasn't sure if I could trust Sang. Oddly, it was his smile that bothered me the most. Was he smiling because he knew he was about to screw his real enemy: Captain Ba and his men, as well as Nogo, Henderson, and me? Or was he trying to comfort me and signal that he understood my dilemma? I asked myself at that point what choice I had and ordered him to tell the captain anyway, saying that I didn't give a flying fuck what Ba wanted to do; my orders were my orders.

An animated conversation between Sang and Captain Ba ensued while I anxiously stood by. When they were finished, Sang glanced at Nogo and Henderson and then elected to address me in French. "Captain Ba has been ordered by Major Thinh to continue the attack. We are to go with him. Your *di wee* has objected, but Major Thinh's plan stands."

I said he couldn't be serious.

"Major Thinh says he has rank, that he's in charge."

"He's fucking crazy," I said. "Does he want to get us all killed?"

Sang simply shrugged like a defeated man.

"Okay," I said. "Here goes nothing." I told Nogo and Henderson to saddle up, that we were moving out.

"What about Sneaky Pete Five?" Nogo asked.

I said to let them know we'd been ordered to attack.

"But, sir, we're headed for a shit sandwich."

"No buts about it, Nogo," I said. "Just do it. And pray for the best."

We proceeded cautiously toward the southern tip of the dense cover that loomed like a solid gray-green wall in the heavy rain. One hundred meters from the tree line Sang said, "Shit. There are no dogs. No water buffaloes. No signs of civilian life. Be prepared, Lieutenant. You were right. We've been set up."

My heart began to race, and each breath felt like a hot belch. This was not what I'd expected, what I'd volunteered for. I frantically signaled to Captain Ba to have his troops take cover, while Sang yelled at him in Vietnamese, but Ba waved us off, and his company of 120 unsuspecting victims, now spread in an erratic line over 250 meters, crossed over the last dike—their last hope of cover—and continued to move forward.

For a moment the howling of the wind stopped, and all was quiet except for the pounding of the rain on the men's helmets and ponchos, and then the tree line erupted with flickering yellow muzzle flashes and the sharp reports of rifles, automatic weapons, and machine guns.

Time seemed to stand still.

Everything moved in slow motion.

The snapping of bullets whizzing overhead sounded as though we'd disturbed a hornets' nest.

Many of the ARVN soldiers were killed or wounded before they could grasp what was happening. The survivors began to return fire and ran and crawled back toward the cover of the dike.

Captain Ba was killed instantly no more than five meters from me.

Two out of three of the ARVN made it safely back to the dike, where they curled beneath the stream of small-arms fire that pinned them in place.

Nogo, Henderson, Sang, and I sprinted for cover, close enough together that we could see the fear and anger in each other's eyes. I doubt that any of us could believe what was happening, that the enemy we'd only known on paper was intent upon killing us, each and every one of us.

Nogo was hit no more than twenty meters from the dike. His body seemed to relax as though all his worldly cares had been lifted from his shoulders, and he fell facedown into the mud, his bulky radio harnessed to his back. I reached for him, but Sang shoved me toward the cover of the dike yelling, "We can't lose you, too."

Henderson was hit in the thigh and dragged himself the final few meters on his elbows and rolled behind the dike. He gave me a quick smile and a thumbs-up and began to bandage his thigh to stem the flow of blood. "Bookoo motherfuckers," he yelled. "Bookoo."

There were cries above the rifle reports of "*Bác sĩ! Bác sĩ!*" and I asked Henderson if he would be able to help with the wounded.

"I hear them callin' for me, sir," he said. "I'll be ready to go most riki tik."

I took a deep breath and wondered if I had the stomach for what I had to do. Had I gotten myself in over my head? Could I really go through with this John Wayne bullshit? I yelled in Sang's ear that I was going back for Nogo. He hollered, "There's no sense going back, Lieutenant. He's gone." But, before he could react, I slipped over the lip of the dike and crawled toward Nogo's motionless form. This was my duty, and I couldn't leave one of my men if he was still alive. And we needed the radio if the rest of us were to survive. As I slithered past two dead or dying ARVN soldiers, something changed. At first I wasn't sure what it was, and then I realized that the staccato rifle reports were even more pronounced because the pounding of the rain had stopped.

I crawled a little farther and grabbed Nogo by his muddy poncho and started to ask if he was with me. The left side of his forehead was shot away, and a leech was crawling up his cheek. From the vacant look in his eyes and the color of his face, the answer was clear, and I felt something I'd never felt before. This was the first time I'd ever seen a dead man, let alone a dead friend. I was shocked and, yes, frightened by the way he looked. What a fucking waste, I thought. I hadn't bargained on this. No way. No fucking way. I pulled the leech from his cheek and made the sign of the cross in front of his chalky face and whispered, "Go in peace, my friend."

I pried the handset from Nogo's tightening grip and struggled to unharness the radio from him. Once it was free, I called Special Forces Command but didn't wait for confirmation of my transmission and asked what had happened to the artillery support, adding that Bravo Company was in deep shit.

"Foxtrot Oscar, this is Sneaky Pete Five actual," came the reply, indicating that it was Captain Frye himself. "There's no one to direct artillery fire. Can you give me coordinates?"

I began to answer when I felt a stinging sensation in my left hand. It took me a few seconds to realize that my pinkie finger had been shot away. It was then that I knew I had to get my act together, to focus on what I was doing. I jammed my hand against my poncho to slow the bleeding, hunched the radio over one shoulder, and had begun to sprint in the sucking footing toward the cover of the dike when I was spun off my feet by a sharp blow to my right shoulder. (The doctors later told me that they guessed it was two or three rounds from an AK-47 that had shattered my shoulder blade and collar bone.) Another shot ricocheted off my helmet, punching it down over my eyes as I dropped to my knees.

For a moment the radio was silent, and then Captain Frye called again, "Foxtrot Oscar, can you read me?"

I fumbled for the handset with my bloody left hand, acknowledged the call, and gathered myself. Tried to assess my wound. But all I could see was a hole as large as a man's fist in my dark green poncho. Hadn't I been warned that the enemy's initial targets would be the radio operator and the officer at his side? "Goddamn son of a bitch," I yelled and told my caller that I'd been hit.

"Can you give me coordinates?" Captain Frye said.

I looked at the handset as though it was a foreign object. Coordinates? The right side of my chest and back were wet and warm with blood. For an instant, the handset went out of focus, and mosquitoes began to swarm around my neck and ears. I pressed the call button and let it go and fell facedown into the mud and rolled on my back. The brightening sky blurred, became clear, and then blurred again. I halfheartedly slapped at the mosquitoes when I heard Captain Frye again. "Foxtrot Oscar, can...you...give...me...coordinates?"

Again I pressed the transmit button, and again I dropped the handset. I watched the sun burn through the gray clouds and wondered if this was the way my unfulfilled life would end, when anger suddenly overcame me and I sat upright. Something told me—I thought I might have even heard a voice—that I *was* invincible, and heard myself scream as though my voice was coming from a faraway place, "You can't kill me, you bastards. No one can take me from Lisette. No one."

I pulled my map from inside my poncho. Blood ran down the upper corner where I held it, and I waited for a moment for the details to come into focus. As I picked the handset from the mud, I looked toward the tree line and watched a green tracer rip the edge of my poncho as calmly as though it were nothing more than a high, inside fastball. Payback time, I thought. This is for you, Nogo. For you, my friend.

My voice was strong and clear and filled with anger. I called in an azimuth and coordinates and an estimated range, and requested a white phosphorous round so I could zero the artillery in. I struggled to remain alert, watched the willy peter round explode on target and radioed, "Bull's-eye! Fire for effect."

I dropped the handset and rolled on my left side to relieve the pressure on my wound. I drew my knees to my chest and lay shivering in the mud. Between the deafening explosions of artillery rounds, I thought I heard the glorious *thump-thump-thump* of approaching helicopters, and I thanked God more than once when—almost as in a dream—I felt a warm rush and heard Henderson say, "There it is, sir. Morphy does the trick every time. Just relax. The dust off will be here most riki tik."

From that point forward, everything seemed to glide across my mental screen in silent, grainy, black and white, and, coming from some faraway place, I heard Henderson's voice again: "An outstanding day for my good lieutenant. A wound that'll get a ticket home and a ride in a Huey." And then I was floating and bumping and rocking on a litter, knowing that I was lucky to be alive, the cold wind of the helicopter's blades blowing on my smiling face.

I remember nothing more until someone tapped my leg. I struggled to move my right arm but couldn't and forced my eyes open. Captain Frye and a smiling Sang stood at the foot of my bed. The captain's voice was barely audible above the sound of the floor fan that slowly rotated back and forth by my bed when he asked, "How you feeling, Lieutenant?"

I studied the olive-drab sling that held my right arm tight against my chest and raised my left hand to inspect its bulky gauze wrapping. Drunkenly I asked, "They find my finger?"

Captain Frye chuckled. "I'm afraid not. The medics had more pressing things to do, like keeping you alive."

I felt my eyelids begin to droop. The captain pressed on my leg to keep me awake. "You're a damn fine soldier, Francis. A lot of men owe their lives to you."

Sang nodded and bowed. "*C'est vrai.*"

I gave a lazy, morphine-induced smile but didn't speak.

Captain Frye laughed. "But someday we'll have to talk about your profanity on the net. You didn't sound like a gentleman graduate of Episcopal to me."

I fought to keep my eyes open and tried to explain. "I'd lost a lot of blood, sir."

"Roger that," the captain said. "You damn near bought the farm."

"What about Nogo?"

Captain Frye shook his head and waited a moment. "I'm sorry, but Nogowski didn't make it. Sang says he was dead before he hit the ground. Do you remember taking his radio?"

"Now I do, sir." My eyes closed. Tears crept down my cheeks, and with them a sense that there was no turning back, that what happened had happened, that it wasn't just a dream. That it was as real as real could be and was something that would always haunt me. "It's just that I never thought I'd lose a buddy…a brother."

"It's a first for me, too," Captain Frye said and came to attention and gave me a smart salute. "Be well, Lieutenant Delafield. I hope our paths cross soon again."

Sang stayed behind while two Thai nurses hovered over me, preparing me for a medevac to the hospital at Clark Field in the Philippines. He glanced at the nurses and switched to French. "Can you hear me?"

I mumbled that I could hear him.

"Major Thinh says that we recovered the VC's radio transmitter and the operation was a success." Sang shrugged. "But at what price? Before you called in the artillery, along with your friend Nogowski, Captain Ba and twelve of his men were killed, and another sixteen were wounded, including your *bác sĩ*." He nodded in the direction of Henderson, who lay snoring heavily in the adjacent bed. "But he'll be okay. He'll be out of here in no time, and I think Captain Frye will send him home with your radio operator's remains."

"I hear you," I said and felt my eyelids slowly lower again.

"One last thing before I lose you," Sang said. "Captain Frye said he doesn't know what the protocol is for you and Henderson being decorated because this was the first time an American has been wounded, and he doubts your army will want to call attention to it. No matter—you're being sent home alive. You're a very lucky man."

He set my father's St. Christopher's medal and two mud-splattered envelopes on the table beside my bed. "We found these in your steel pot and your fatigues. Maybe someday you will find the letters interesting reading."

I thanked him and said I'd shake his hand, if only I could.

Sang smiled. "That's okay." He leaned over and held an open hand against my cheek. "Good-bye, Lieutenant. I pray you heal quickly."

Valley Forge General Hospital

My memories of my stay at the Clark Field hospital are much like the morphine-induced nightmares I experienced there: they come and go in waves. While it was a time of a lot of pain, sweat-soaked bedclothes from the insufferable heat, and delicate care from a small band of beautiful Philippine nurses, until I was strong enough to walk, my lone connection to the air base and its surroundings was a small window that looked out at the stilted, thatched-roof houses that dotted the rice paddies in the distance. I stared through that window for hours on end watching water buffaloes trudge back and forth in the muck, seemingly as bored as I was.

Those were some of the longest and most depressing days I've ever experienced; I was logy and without energy from the heat and pain killers, and I couldn't seem to finish a thought or bring clarity to anything as I struggled to make sense of what was in store for me when I was sent back to the States. Nogo's death continued to haunt me, making it more difficult for me to come to grips with why I'd volunteered for Vietnam in the first place. I continually wondered whether or not I should make the army a career, or if I should go back to Dartmouth, or…I couldn't think of too many other options. What was most disturbing of all, however, was the question of what I should do about Lisette and how to do it. But every time it seemed that I might be close to a decision, I would drift off into fitful, sweaty sleep.

In August I was rotated back to Valley Forge General Hospital to undergo reconstructive surgery on my shoulder. The army thought it was doing me a favor by sending me to Valley Forge because it was no more than an hour from my family in Chestnut Hill. As it turned out, I could have been in a hospital in Timbuktu given the number of visits from my parents, their first being the day after I arrived from the Philippines, a few days before my scheduled surgery. My father was smiling as he hurried into my room. My mother, in a navy suit, high heels, and pillbox hat, looked as though she was on her way to a Friday afternoon concert of the orchestra and, before saying a word, gave an imperious wave, dismissing the nurse who had been attending to me.

Dad reached to shake my hand and then realized that my right arm was in a sling and gently squeezed my left hand, careful to avoid the bandage where my pinkie finger used to be. "Welcome home, Lieutenant," he said. "You in a lot of pain?"

I told him it could be worse.

Mom kissed me lightly on the cheek and said, "What are they feeding you? You're almost *squelettique*."

"I haven't felt much like eating," I said. "I'm sure that'll change after the operation."

"Well, I certainly hope so," she said and looked at my father. "Perhaps we should call Tom Gates—"

"Mom, I'll be fine," I interrupted. "There's no need to call anyone, certainly not Mr. Gates."

Tom Gates was deputy secretary of defense at the time, on his way to becoming the secretary, and was an old friend of my parents from Chestnut Hill. I thought he was the last person on earth who needed to hear that I wasn't getting enough to eat in a

VA hospital. Dad appeared to agree and said that he didn't think it was in Tom's job description. Then he hurriedly changed the subject, saying, "Heather will be here tomorrow with Potter. We didn't want to overwhelm you with too many visitors on your first day home."

"You are coming home, aren't you?" my mother asked. "I mean, you don't plan on making the military a career, do you?"

I said I didn't know what I was going to do, that I'd make up my mind once I'd been discharged from the hospital.

"Oh?" Mom said. "Everyone hopes you'll go back to Dartmouth."

"I know. I know," I said, "but right now I'm taking things one day at a time."

Mom glanced at Dad and then spoke in French. "I hope you'll do what's expected of you."

I told her not to worry, that I'd do my best.

My father smiled. "You certainly did in Vietnam."

"But at what cost?" my mother asked and raised a hand to Dad before he could answer. "Thank heavens all of this will soon be forgotten." She looked at her watch. "I'm afraid we must go. Good luck with your operation and remember…" She paused as though she was weighing what to say next and then shook her head and said, "No. That's all." She kissed me good-bye and again wished me *bonne chance.*

My father squeezed my good shoulder. "Hang in there, Son. This is a tough time, but brighter days lie ahead. I know what it's like to have to deal with the end of your tour, but I'm pretty sure everything will work out."

The visit from Heather and Potter was both joyous and trouble-some: joyous because it reminded me how much I cared for them; troublesome because it made me realize that their lives had grown far apart from mine, that we now had so little in common that, no matter how hard I tried, they'd never understand what I'd experienced.

Heather talked excitedly about her job at the art museum. As always she was entertaining, especially when she described the brief period after she'd graduated from Vassar when she lived at Twelve-Twelve, referring to it as "the block house" as though it were some kind of penitentiary. She also complained that all the guys she'd been dating seemed to have been stamped out of the same stuffy WASP cookie cutter.

As for Potter, he was anxious to start his senior year at Princeton (which had taken him back after his six months with the City Troop) and hoped that he hadn't bitten off more than he could chew by becoming president of the Ivy Club, singing with the Tigertones, Princeton's a capella group, and captaining the tennis team. But—Potter being Potter—what seemed to interest him most was a girl; in this case his new stepsister, a legacy of his father's recent, and fourth, marriage.

As I listened to Heather and Potter talk about lives that were so foreign to mine, I wondered where I belonged. All I had at the time was a shot-up shoulder from a war no one seemed to give a damn about. On top of that, one of the things that bothered me most was that, by the time I was to be discharged, most of my friends would have already graduated from college, and some would have married or gone to graduate school or both, while I would be nothing more than a twenty-three-year-old divorcé with a high school diploma.

Those facts created a gap that I had no idea how to close. And, while I knew this was something that I was going to have to deal with sooner or later, at the time I thought maybe the generals who had tried to sell me on making the army a career were right: maybe the army *was* the place for me.

Shortly after Heather and Potter said good-bye, I received a surprise visit from Dr. Ames, who carried a gift-wrapped package in one hand and a thick folder of medical files in the other. Before he even said hello, he told me that finding someone in this rabbit warren of a hospital was like finding a needle in a haystack, that it was the biggest, most confusing damn hospital he'd ever seen, and then he handed me the package. "Here's something for you to read while you're recuperating. I think you'll enjoy it."

I struggled to undo the wrapping with my bandaged hand and finally got the book free and studied its cover: *The Atlantic Salmon* by Lee Wulff. "It's kind of the bible," Dr. Ames said. "I hope it'll encourage you to fish with me again, once you're back on your feet."

I thanked him and said I'd like that very much.

"Good," Dr. Ames said and tapped the overflowing folder. "I've reviewed your files with your surgeon. He was a classmate at medical school, and rest assured, Fran, you're in the best of hands. You may not be throwing fastballs when you get out of here, but you should be able to do everything else, including cast a fly."

I had often wondered if I would ever be able to pitch again, but the other doctors I'd discussed the subject with had offered nothing more than a cautious "let's wait and see." I knew that Dr. Ames would be honest with me and tried to downplay my anxiety by forcing a smile as I asked, "You mean I'll have to become a knuckleballer?"

Dr. Ames was slow to answer as he slipped the folder into the file holder at the foot of my bed. "Sorry, Fran, but I'm afraid your baseball days are over. Stranger things have happened, but the odds aren't in your favor." He smiled his slow, warm smile. "More importantly, let's hope all goes well tomorrow. And read the book, but don't expect another thirty-six-pound salmon."

I corrected him. "Thirty-seven."

He chuckled, said he had to run, and waved good-bye, but I was preoccupied with his prognosis for my shoulder. I tried to imagine how much fun it would be to return to Dartmouth, or go to any college for that matter, if I couldn't play baseball. It was just one more thing to wrestle with during the long days I'd spend recuperating.

———∞∞∞———

According to my surgeon, the operation was a success, and, with rigorous rehab, I should "eventually return to a normal range of motion, but not the motion required to throw a fastball or a curve." With that short, clinical evaluation, my baseball dreams came to an end. Even though it took me a long time to accept it, I struggled to put it behind me as quickly as I could, for I knew that my next task was developing a new life plan—a plan that began with making contact with René.

I called the international operator and asked for information in La Malbaie. After a moment a woman came on the line and said, "Good day. This is La Malbaie. How may I help you?"

Good God, I thought. That voice is familiar. Of course. The town telephone operator. My heart began to race. "Lisette?"

The operator paused. "Excuse me?"

"Lisette, it's me."

There was a long silence. "This is La Malbaie. How may I help you?"

"Lisette, it's me. Fran."

"I'm sorry," the operator said. "I do not understand. How may I direct your call?"

I let out a long breath. I thought for sure I was talking to the woman I loved. "Come on, Lisette. We must talk. This is our chance. Enough time must have passed."

"There must be some mistake."

"Of course," I mumbled. "A mistake. A huge mistake if you won't talk to me. Please, Lisette, we now have a chance to get back together. To make all that's changed worth our while."

"I'm sorry, sir, but I do not know a Lisette." I couldn't believe what I was hearing. "Now, how may I help you? There are other calls waiting."

"I'll bet there are," I said in English and sighed. "I'm trying to get the phone number for a Monsieur René Jaud."

The operator said she didn't have a listing for that name and asked if there was anything else she could do for me.

"Yes," I said and thought the least she could do would be to talk to me or give me a signal of some kind. Now that I had the freedom to remarry her, what could stand in our way? A life with Lisette was how I'd imagined my future. I wondered how this had gone so wrong—so terribly wrong—and what I could have done differently. And why nothing in my life would stand still. "Please tell Lisette that I love her very much and always will," I said and hung up.

Fini

During my recuperation, along with all the get-well cards from family and friends, I received two letters that would shape my future. The first was postmarked Cincinnati, smelled of perfume, and had been forwarded from 1212 Poor Richard's Lane. I didn't recognize the name of the sender and didn't think I knew anyone who lived in Ohio. I turned the envelope over, and the familiar prep-school notation *SWAK*—*sealed with a kiss*—was written across the back and I wondered, "Who the hell is this?"

> *Dear Fran,*
>
> *I'm sure getting a letter from some strange woman named Putnam may make you want to pee your pants, but don't; it's me, Bar Wainwright. As you can guess, I'm an old married lady now and have moved with my hubby, Mike Putnam, to Cincinnati where he's started in the training program at P & G. It's all very exciting and lots of hard work and we're expecting our first baby in February!*
>
> *But that's not why I'm writing. I hear you're a war hero and were wounded in Vietnam. How scary is*

*that? My father says we need more young men like you.
Mike thinks you're nuts for doing what you did, but
admitted to me the other day that he includes you in
his prayers, mostly because he played tennis with Potter
at Princeton and Potter told him you're a really good
egg. I worry about you, too, and hope you'll be okay.*

*I heard all this from Maisie Bingham who keeps track
of you and wonders if you remember her from my party.
From what she's told me, that night would be hard to forget!
Anyhoo, she's still single and works in New York for Christie's.
If you'd ever like to see her again, you can call her at work.*

*I don't spend a lot of time playing Cupid but Maisie's a
dear friend and—she'd kill me for telling you this—she has a
real sneaker for you.*

*Well, that's all for now, except I can't
tell you how proud I am of you.*

Buckets of love and get well soon.

xxx ooo

Bar

The few times that I'd thought about Maisie Bingham and the night
we'd met, I'd wished it was nothing more than a drunken nightmare, that it hadn't really happened. So, "thanks, but no thanks"
was my reaction to Bar's offer. Debutantes like Maisie were a dime
a dozen, and, besides, our night together had the opposite impact
on me. Perhaps it was because of my regrets and my feelings of
shame and infidelity to Lisette, but for me it was a night I'd sooner
forget.

A month later I received a letter from René, a letter I couldn't open
quickly enough. René's petite, stylized script barely covered the
single pale blue page.

My dear friend—

Wonderful news! M. Trudeau has just learned
from Potter's father that you are back from Vietnam
and are recuperating near your home in Pennsylvania.
I hope your operation was a success and that you
soon can get on with the next chapter in your life.

I have some sad news to share. Babette died of pan-
creatic cancer last summer but, as I write you, I have
a three-month-old miniature poodle nestled in my lap.
He is named Boom Boom after the great Geoffrion and
is slowly replacing Babette's place in my heart. Isn't it
wonderful how the human spirit heals over time?

I hope we can renew our friendship and that we will
meet again on the St. Jean although, since our trip, the
fishing has steadily deteriorated. Something must be done
to reverse the trend or in a few years there won't be any
salmon left, certainly none as large as your great fish.

To your good health,
René

I stared at the letter and the phone number that he'd written at the bottom of the page. I couldn't believe what René had written: news about fishing and his goddamned dog, but not a word about Lisette. What was this, some kind of a cruel joke? A conspiracy? Had Lisette told him that I'd called to find his phone number? I reread the letter, focusing on his question: "Isn't it wonderful how the human spirit heals over time?" Was he trying to tell me something to prepare me for some really bad news?

I knew René would be expecting my call and spoke in English to let him know that I wasn't pleased with his letter.

"Ah, my dear Fran, how is your shoulder?" he asked.

I told him that it was healing on schedule, that it should be almost as good as new, and thanked him for his concern. "But, René, you didn't write one word about Lisette. Why not? Is she all right? Is something wrong?"

"I assume everything is fine. I have not heard to the contrary. As I told you, she has moved from La Malbaie."

"She hasn't moved, René, so don't give me that bullshit. I talked to her when I tried to get your number."

"Impossible."

"Okay, play your little game if you must, but what can you tell me? Has she remarried? And what about our baby? Surely your brother has kept you informed."

René made his familiar *pfiff* sound. "Interestingly, he has not, or perhaps I should say, *did* not. He disowned Lisette when she came home from the States and would not speak to her, or of her. But, as you say, that's water over the dam. He was killed in a hunting accident last fall, but even that is not important. What is important is that you accept that things between Lisette and you are over. You must understand that, Fran. You simply must. You signed the papers. She was committed to putting you and your parents behind her and starting anew. She told me she couldn't face the pain of falling in love with you again and maybe losing you again. So, please, leave her alone. I very much want you both to be happy. She is like a daughter to me, and you a son, and I am convinced that that is what's best for you both."

"But what about the baby?" I said. "You've got to tell me, René. She took my father's money. What did she do?"

"I am afraid I cannot answer that, other than to say that it was a very difficult, painful time for her." He sighed, and I thought maybe he would go further until he said, "My advice may be very French, but it is good nonetheless: cultivate your own garden, Fran. Worry about yourself and about making a new life, and not about Lisette and her situation. Worry about returning to college or whatever you do next. What's done is done, and you cannot reverse it. As one door closes, another opens."

There was a sincerity to René's tone that I had heard only once before, when he'd pledged to be my friend, and I believed that he was trying to do what was best for Lisette, and for me. I spoke in French, the language of our friendship. "Is that what you were hinting at when you wrote how wonderful it is that the human spirit heals over time?"

"I guess," René said.

"You're sure it's over? That this is what she wants? What she really wants, René? What's really best?"

"Yes, yes, and yes," René answered. "It is unbelievably difficult and sad, but you are so young and have so much opportunity in front of you. I pray every night to Saint Sophia that I am right, that I am helping you both. So please, Fran, move on and, when you are healed, come fishing. Come see me."

For the next two months, during the long periods of boredom and physical therapy, I wrestled with René's advice, trying to convince myself that it was for the best, that it was over between Lisette and me. *Fini*.

Fini, goddamn it. *Fini*.

<hr />

In November, with my shoulder on the mend, I was reassigned to the 10th Special Forces where I was deskbound, doing boring, repetitive administrative work while waiting for my enlistment to come to an end. In December I became a first lieutenant, and finally, in April 1960, after I'd served a little over four years in the army, I was honorably discharged. Not only that, my debt to Dad had been paid in full, and I had close to $2,000 in the bank.

The day before I mustered out, I was summoned—somewhat mysteriously, I thought—to a meeting with General Sink, the commandant of the XVIII Airborne Corps. Besides the fact that he was severe looking and an airborne legend, he was a three-star general, and I'd never talked to a man of his rank before. After I saluted and reported to him, he walked around his desk and greeted me with a handshake. In his thick southern drawl, he said he had a pleasant surprise for me and told me to come to attention. As I did, a photographer walked into the office and moved in front of us. General Sink acknowledged him with a slight nod and said to me, "Congratulations, Lieutenant, it is my great pleasure and honor to award you a Silver Star for gallantry and a Purple Heart." As he draped the medals around my neck, he said, "I apologize that these awards are so long overdue, but our command in Vietnam wasn't really sure how to handle your situation and argued it to death. Finally, they all agreed, and the ARVN—I would guess not to be outdone by us—has awarded you a Presidential Unit Citation and their Gallantry Cross, also with a silver star." He shook my hand again, patted me on the shoulder, and almost in a whisper said, "At ease."

We posed for a few more pictures, and then the general dismissed the photographer and turned to me. "Are you sure you want to leave us? It's not too late to change your mind, you know. I'd be delighted if you decided to re-up."

I told him that it was a very difficult decision for me (true), that I'd wrestled with it many times (also true), but that I wanted to complete my college education and then I might consider reenlisting (kind of true).

"A sound plan, young man," the general said. "I like it. Major Frye tells me that you're a damn fine soldier, and I do hope you'll rejoin us someday." He paused. "And, yes, he's *Major* Frye now and is in charge of all airborne operations at Nha Trang." He paused again and smiled for the first time. "Someday, Francis, that could be you."

"I think I'd like that, sir," I said. "Maybe someday. Yes, sir. Maybe someday."

But all I knew for sure as I left the general's office was that a career in the army was on hold because something deep down was calling me to come home. But, without Lisette and any firm plans, I had no idea what for.

1960

Reentry

Perhaps it was nothing more than the beginning of my adjustment to civilian life, but that first night at home, I felt invisible, like I'd crashed the party but no one had noticed. To begin, I was struck by how nothing had changed and yet how different everything looked, even smelled, from the way I remembered. The lithograph of Carroll Tyson's angry great blue heron fighting with a snake—a wedding present to Mom and Dad from the artist—still hung to the left of the fireplace, while the family heirloom, the somewhat lugubrious portrait by Robert Edge Pine of Francis Hopkinson holding a quill and staring vacantly off into space, was hung to the right. Yet now, both looked oddly out of place. Too symmetrical? Too familiar? Too suggestive of the past? I wasn't sure.

The bulky Philco television set was, as always, positioned in front of the armchair that acted as Dad's refuge from family squabbles (and where Red Skelton, Jack Benny, and Jackie Gleason often amused him, and where, for reasons best known to Dad, Ed Sullivan annoyed him on a weekly basis), but that night the TV and the armchair looked shopworn and abandoned, as though they'd been left at the curb for the trash men to collect. Even the butler's table, with the signatures of Dad's ushers engraved on a sheet of brass in its center, looked unpolished and no longer cared for.

When I carried my duffel bag to my bedroom, that most familiar of rooms didn't feel quite right either. It was far less welcoming and more sparsely decorated than I remembered it being when Lisette and I had spent our single week of marriage there, and I wondered if Mom had rearranged it to erase any reminders of her embarrassment.

Further, my parents seemed more anxious than usual to start their cocktail hour promptly at six thirty. They'd been seated on their favorite couch for only a few moments, my mother nervously stirring her old-fashioned, and Dad—who was by then officially "on the wagon"—nursing a tall glass of tonic water, when the front door opened and a voice called, "This the Chestnut Hill VFW?"

It was Potter, and his presence instantly eased the tension. He kissed Mom and Heather, shook Dad's hand, and locked me in a bear hug. When he finally let go, he introduced us all to his new stepsister, Deirdre Dunning, who stood patiently at the edge of the scene, smiling a brilliant smile. I thought Potter had been right when he'd written me that she was tall, willowy, and almost white-blond, and hadn't been nicknamed "Stunning Dunning" for nothing.

The conversation at cocktails and dinner, as conversations frequently did with my mother, began with her checking Deirdre's pedigree: where she grew up (Tuxedo Park), where she'd gone to school and college (Westover and Smith), and what she was doing now (debating going to Le Cordon Bleu in Paris to learn to cook).

When the questioning turned to Potter, he said that he'd just been accepted by the Wharton School. Before I could congratulate him, Mom turned to me and said, "You see, Fran, even your friends seem to agree that a college degree, perhaps even a postgraduate degree, is necessary."

Heather held her fork in midair and glared at Mom. "This is about Potter's good news," she said in French, "not about whether or not Franny goes to college, if you please."

"None of that tonight," Dad said in an uncharacteristically firm voice. "Tonight's a night for celebrating having our son home at last." He raised his glass of tonic to me. "We're so proud of you and so happy to have you with us in the bosom of the family once again."

"But certainly, Theo, this is a subject we should discuss," Mom said.

"I agree, Gay," Dad said, "but not tonight."

An awkward silence settled over the table until Heather asked if anyone would like seconds. When I said that I would, Potter said he would, too, and followed me to the kitchen. "You get the picture?" I said. "Mom won't let this college thing alone for love nor money."

As I began to ladle stew onto Potter's plate, he held my hand in place. "Don't worry, Delafield, shit like that happens with every-body's parents. If you don't believe me, when we get back to the table, ask if I have any more news. My answer's going to make your family look like Ted Mack's *Amateur Hour*."

I hesitated and then asked the obvious question: "Deidre pregnant?"

"Nope. I learned my lesson long ago on that score. It's more complicated than that." He turned to leave the kitchen, and then stopped. "We're getting married." He shook his head as though he was as amazed by the news as I was. "Can you beat that? It'll give our parents' friends something to talk about for months."

"I take it this is good news," I said.

"Not good news, Delafield. Great news. Fabulous news. But Deidre and I are going to need all the friends we've got."

Once back in the dining room, I asked Potter, as casually as I could, what else was new. He looked at Deirdre, who nodded at him with the hint of a smile. "Well," he said and paused.

"Go on, Potter," Deirdre said. "There's no time like the present."

While I waited for Potter to speak, I could see him at the foot of my bed in La Malbaie with a Hudson Bay blanket drawn across his shoulders trying to gather his courage to tell me that Sidney was pregnant, and he looked as uncomfortable at this moment as he did then. "Well," he said again, "it's top secret for a little while longer, but Deirdre and I are getting married."

"Holy shit!" Heather said. "Sorry, Daddy, but she's his—"

"I assume your father and your stepmother are delighted," Mom interrupted. From her tone there was no doubt that she didn't think the Morrises would be delighted, and that she wouldn't be either.

Potter wiped his mouth with his napkin. "Not exactly, Mrs. Delafield. That's why you're the first people we've told. I guess you could say you're kind of our guinea pigs." He laughed what I thought was an unnatural laugh for him. "My old man views Deirdre and me as brother and sister and calls what we're doing 'borderline incestuous.' The good news is, Deirdre's mom agrees with us. She says we're just two unrelated people who fell in love." Potter looked at everyone at the table, one by one. "So, the sixty-four-thousand-dollar question is, is Dad overreacting, or are we going to be the laughingstock of Philadelphia?"

"A juicy topic at first, for sure," Heather said, "but when people have had time to think about it, it'll be okay and soon forgotten."

I agreed and added that if they were happy, who cared what people thought?

"Listen to you, Heather and Fran," Mom said. "You are so naïve. It *does* make a difference what people think, what Potter's father thinks."

Heather muttered, "Up to a point. After that, *chacun ses goûts.*"

Potter glanced at Deirdre and then asked my father what he thought.

"I think Fran's right," Dad said.

Mom started to say something, but Dad interrupted her. "Please, Gay, let me finish." He smiled at Deirdre and Potter. "Mrs. Delafield's right: perception is always important, but in the end, happiness trumps all."

I looked at Heather and cleared my throat.

"What?" Potter asked.

"Nothing," I said, wondering where my father had been when I needed support like that with Lisette.

A week later, Potter and Deirdre announced their engagement and set their wedding date for late June, all with great fanfare and very little tongue wagging. Somewhere along the line, Mr. Morris changed his tune, perhaps because his new wife so adamantly supported her daughter and Potter. That support for their kids remained another sore point with me for a long, long time, as did Potter's being accepted by Wharton. It seemed to open Pandora's box for me, and my college plans became a nightly topic of discussion. The issue finally came to a head when I said that I'd decided not to go back to Dartmouth, at least not in the near future, because I wasn't sure of the value of a college degree and was worried that I'd fallen too far behind my friends to have my future slowed by four years in college.

My mother sipped her old-fashioned, and my father stared at his glass of tonic water. Both smoked, but neither spoke. It was as though they hadn't understood what I had said; it was reminiscent of all the many discussions I'd had with them about other decisions of mine that hadn't pleased them. Finally, Dad asked, "Exactly what was it you didn't like about Dartmouth?"

"It's not Dartmouth," I said. "Under normal circumstances I think I would have been very happy there, but now—and I'm sure Mom and you won't agree—I can't help but wonder if college isn't just another one-size-fits-all social custom. What's more, I got a great sense of satisfaction from my army pay and my ability to settle my debts with you, Dad, and I don't know if I really want to go another four years without that feeling of independence."

My mother looked blankly at me and clumsily stubbed out her cigarette and handed Dad her empty glass. "There must be something else, Theo. Perhaps quitting Dartmouth for no good reason has something to do with it. Perhaps he's embarrassed."

Dad gave me a curious look and stood, but before heading for the bar, he asked if I had thought this decision all the way through, saying that sooner or later my friends would have to fulfill some form of military obligation that would put them on more even footing with me. He gave me a kind smile and said, "Look. You've distinguished yourself as a baseball player and as a soldier, so now would be a good time for you to broaden your intellectual horizons before distinguishing yourself in another field."

I was speechless. It was the first time I could remember my father saying something flattering or supportive since I'd gone away to Episcopal. I was both stunned and encouraged, and I hoped that it meant we could get things back on track, that I could discuss things with him rather than arguing every point.

While Dad mixed Mom's cocktail, she spoke in French, saying that my father was being way too lenient with me, that he wasn't firm enough, and that his permissiveness had not served him well with me or at his office. She lit another cigarette and said that I must get a college degree, that it was expected of boys like me.

Garçons comme moi? She had to be kidding. I was twenty-three, had already been married and divorced, and had just been awarded one of our armed forces' highest decorations for valor, and she thought of me as a boy?

I bit my tongue and told her that I'd give the topic some more thought.

Blind Date

Putting aside my mother's insensitive comment about *garçons comme moi*, I reapplied to Dartmouth. But I also began to search for a job, temporary as it might be, but one that someday might lead to a career and the potential for some big paydays. Because I had no idea where to start, I sought advice from a few of Dad's friends. Based on their experiences after their war, all assumed that my military record would be a huge plus, and all agreed that if I didn't go back to college, the best avenue for me to pursue was sales.

Consequently, I interviewed at Scott Paper (the only open sales territories were in Chillicothe, Ohio, and Lubbock, Texas), the Tasty Baking Company (cutting back their sales force; not hiring at that time), and the local pharmaceutical company, Smith, Kline & French (the open territory in the Philadelphia area required a college degree, and the company had a strong preference for married men with sales experience).

I also talked with a number of insurance companies and brokerage houses, with little success. It turned out that Dad's friends' assumptions that my experience in Vietnam would be helpful were outdated. Perhaps even more than just outdated, because not only did the personnel executives I talked with seem confused by my involvement in a war they knew nothing about and that many had never even heard of, but I sensed an undercurrent of disapproval. Further, most ended my interview by encouraging me to finish my education and then reapply.

Surprisingly, Dartmouth also rejected me. The letter was short but not so sweet: "Your inexplicable disappearance in the fall of 1955 after the college had awarded you a generous scholarship and had maintained high hopes for you both in the classroom and on the baseball diamond has left a bitter taste in our collective mouths, and we think a different institution where you could start afresh would be better for all concerned."

At the height of my confusion and despair, a friend of my father's tried to sell me on joining his brokerage firm. He promised that he would turn several accounts over to me to get me started as he transitioned toward retirement. He also promised that if I worked as hard as he knew I would—as anyone with my military training and experience would—I'd be making six figures in no time.

So, late in the summer of 1960, I joined W. H. Newbold's Son & Company and celebrated my financial independence by renting a one-room walk-up in west Philadelphia. It was a cramped space, for sure, but one I could call my own, and it got me out from under the critical watch of my parents. And, as the man who hired me had predicted, thanks to the risk-taking customers whose accounts he'd switched over to me, in time I began to make more money than I'd ever dreamed I would.

<hr />

The big national news in the fall of 1960 was that Jack Kennedy had been elected president. It upset my parents no end because they hated JFK's father and were suspicious of anyone who was a Democrat, let alone a Democrat *and* a Catholic. As Mom not so delicately put it, "Choate never would have accepted those Kennedy boys if their father hadn't given the school so much money. They must have been the very first Catholics to go there and, I would guess, the last." (With this as our family's stated political position, it was no wonder that neither Heather nor I ever admitted that we'd voted for Kennedy.)

On Thanksgiving Day, I sprained my ankle badly in a touch football game and ended up on crutches for six weeks. But, other than that, things fell into a comfortable routine for me until mid-December when Potter called and said he had some news he thought would make me happy. I thought for sure he was going to tell me that Deirdre was pregnant. Instead he said that his father had been offered tickets by one of his suppliers for the championship game between the Eagles and the Green Bay Packers and asked if I would like to go with him. I jumped at the chance, and the day after Christmas, Potter and Deirdre met me outside Franklin Field shortly before kickoff. As they greeted me, someone standing behind me put their hands over my eyes and whispered in my ear, "Surprise!" and turned me toward her. "It's Maisie Bingham. Remember?"

At first I was put off by Potter and Deirdre setting me up with someone whom I really didn't care to ever see again, but the embarrassed tone in which Maisie asked if I remembered her encouraged me to give her a second chance. (Potter later confessed that he and Deirdre had been scheming for months to fix me up with Maisie, and when his dad offered him tickets to the game, Potter knew that the opportunity they'd been looking for had arrived. "Gotcha, Delafield," was his summary. "Gotcha but good.")

After the game, with Maisie following, I hopped up the two dimly lit flights of stairs to my apartment, grabbing the banister with one hand, clutching my crutches in the other. "Wow, this really *is* a broom closet!" Maisie giggled as I ushered her in. "The bed doubles for a couch? How the heck do you entertain?"

"No one ever comes here but me," I said.

Maisie raised an eyebrow. "No one?"

"No one I could take home to my mother."

"You still hung up on that?" she asked.

"Was I when—"

"Yes," Maisie said, "but that's ancient history. Or at least I hope it is."

She pulled off her coat, sat on the edge of the bed, and unzipped her fleece-lined stadium boots and kicked out of them. She set them neatly at the end of the bed and stretched her legs, moving her feet in small circles. I couldn't help but notice what great, athletic legs she had and realized that I couldn't remember much about her body from our night together. As though she sensed what I was thinking, she smiled at me and patted the bed, inviting me to sit. "Can we talk?"

I hesitated and asked if she'd like something to drink. "No, thanks," she said and patted the bed again. "Not to worry, I won't bite you."

I leaned my crutches against the desk and sat next to her, resting my injured leg on the desk chair. "I guess Potter must have sold you pretty hard to come all the way from New York just to see a football game," I said.

"I didn't come to watch football. I came to explain some stuff to you."

I scratched my pant leg at the top of my cast but didn't speak.

Maisie held my hand in place. "Relax, Fran, I'm not the nympho you think I am—that everybody says I am."

I started to say something, but she wagged a finger at me. "You don't have to say anything. I wouldn't blame you no matter what you think of me after what we did at Bar's party." She patted my hand in a motherly fashion. "So, please, listen up. I've got something I'd like to tell you, so let me get through this, okay?" She paused as though she was waiting for my permission to continue, then said, "Sex was so new and naughty that summer, and half the thrill of it was doing it where I might get caught or doing it with someone who couldn't afford to get caught, so it was titillating in more ways than one. It was crazy fun. Super, crazy fun. But after that night at Bar's, I couldn't stop wondering why you didn't come back for more. Every other guy did. And I kind of got obsessed by you saying nice things about me and couldn't get the way you held me before you ran away out of my head. And then, after I'd heard you were a big hero, I began to think about you even more."

I lifted her hand and moved it back and forth between us as though I was trying to generate what to say. "I'm no different now than when we met, Maisie, and I'm no hero, that's for sure. I was only in Vietnam for a few months, and what happened—the fire-fight—lasted all of about fifteen, no more than twenty, minutes." I shrugged. "I'm just like the other guys who did crazy things that seemed heroic. We'd have been ashamed of ourselves if we didn't. What we were most afraid of was letting each other know how afraid we really were. I guess you can say we were afraid to be afraid. In my case, I think I was afraid of failing, too."

She muttered, "Wow."

"Yeah, wow," I said. "Besides, I was *dinky dau*—crazy—with the loss of blood and thought I had someone looking out for me."

"Someone?"

I nodded.

"Like God?"

"Who knows? I don't really remember much of it except that I was crazy enough to think that the Viet Cong couldn't kill me." I paused and felt my eyes begin to fill with tears. "The way they got Nogo."

"Nogo? Is that a person?"

I nodded. "One of my men, and a damn good guy. He was only twenty and was going to get married as soon as he got home."

"That's horrible," Maisie said. "You miss him?"

"Yes," I said. "But I miss a lot of people."

For a moment neither of us spoke. Finally, Maisie took my hand with the missing pinkie and inspected it. "That was part of it?"

I sighed as I tried to put my thoughts about Nogo behind me. "Yup, the easy part. My shoulder was the hard part."

"So I've heard. It's the pits. That's why I hate war so much." She paused for a moment. "Well, I just wanted you to know that I've changed a lot since we were together too, but, unlike you, I didn't get wounded. Instead I hurt someone else, a really nice guy who lost his wife and his two kids because of me." She looked at me and gave me a pained smile. "So that's it, and I doubt I'll ever live it down. I'll never forgive myself, and apparently lots of other people won't either." She set my hand on my thigh and patted it one last time. "There. That's it. That's what I wanted to tell you."

Frankly, I didn't know how to respond. Finally I said, "It takes two to tango."

"No one seems to care," Maisie said.

"What'd your parents do, disown you?"

"Half and half. They were going through an ugly divorce at the time, and Dad was living with his girlfriend and being a real jerk, pretending that my stuff never happened. He just kind of dropped off the face of the earth. Mom, on the other hand, wanted to disown me at first, but eventually came around to being my greatest defender. I think that's what grew me up. She was so understanding. She thought I might have been reacting to what Dad had done, or that I was just reacting to everything…you know…all her and Dad's shit. So she took part of the blame, and we talked a lot. And I mean a lot. And finally I saw—understood, really—how badly I'd screwed up. I'd guess that's the way your parents have been with all you've been through."

I flinched at her comment, wondering if she knew more about me, maybe even somehow about Lisette and me, than she should. She gave me a quizzical look. "Is there something more?"

"Than what?"

"Than quitting Dartmouth and getting wounded?"

"Oh," I said. "Well yes, but that's a whole other story."

She looked at her watch. "Maybe some other time? If I hurry, I can catch the seven o'clock." She zipped on her boots, stood, and picked up her coat. "Here's the other thing I wanted to tell you. If we ever find ourselves, you know, doing what we did at Bar's party again, it'll be because we mean something to each other. Okay? I'm a different girl now."

"Roger that," I said. I struggled to stand and gain my balance and helped her into her coat. She turned to me, pinching her gloves together in her left hand in much the same fashion I'd seen my mother adopt many times before. She reached to shake hands. "Friends?"

"Friends."

"Will you call me?"

"Even better," I said. "If you could catch a later train, I'll buy you dinner."

She smiled and said there was a train a little before ten, that it was a milk run, but she thought it would work fine. Just fine.

The Early 1960's

Two for the Price of One

1963. Potter and Deirdre's surprise had its intended effect. Maisie and I discovered that we had lots of fun together and shared many things in common, not the least of which was that we were both trying to live down our teenage reputations. As a result, on Halloween 1962, my engagement to Mary Ault Bingham was announced in the society sections of the Philadelphia papers and the *New York Times* and *Herald Tribune*, and the following June 22nd we were married in Christ Church in Greenwich in front of three hundred of the Binghams' and my parents' most intimate friends.

Maisie was a knockout. Her smile, her blue eyes that always seemed to be laughing at something, and the faint splash of freckles across her nose and cheeks that I'd admired when we first met made her irresistible. And, as a pleasant surprise for her, her father briefly came back into her life to give her away and seemed genuinely moved by the experience.

With Potter as my best man, Bar Putnam as Maisie's maid of honor, and Heather a bridesmaid, even though the wedding ceremony and reception was a lavish production by Philadelphia standards, I must admit that I was comfortable with the whole deal, even though I'd turned my back on all of that type of thing several years before.

While Maisie had the right pedigree and all the proper social boxes checked, marrying her wasn't without its complications—mostly thanks to my mother. Even though it was the only time Maisie was involved with a married man, Mom continued to harbor not particularly well-hidden, negative feelings about the marriage she'd disrupted. And, as frustrating as it was, I never was able to get Mom to accept—and understand—that it was the marriage Maisie *helped* disrupt and that there definitely were two sides to that story. I kept telling her that Maisie was only eighteen, for God's sake, and the guy was twenty-six and should have known better. But all my arguments fell on deaf ears.

No matter. Maisie's "home wrecker" reputation stuck with her, as did rumors of her sexual promiscuity—not only with Mom but with many of her friends. As a result, both Maisie and I were sensitive to the Chestnut Hill crowd's critical eyes and put down our roots across the river in a teeny house on the outskirts of Bryn Mawr.

The first few years of our marriage seemed to blend one year into the next. Our weekday routine included eating supper on TV tables—we were addicted to shows like *Dr. Kildare*, *The Smothers Brothers*, and *Laugh-In*—and every Friday and Saturday night, we went to a friend's house where almost everyone had a number of drinks before dinner. (After I got out of the army, I became a beer drinker because by then Dad was on the wagon, and I thought giving up the hard stuff would support him in what I assumed was his effort to not contribute to Mom's problem. But, like with so many things at the time, Dad and I seemed to travel parallel tracks, and, although Mom's drinking became progressively worse, he never discussed the subject with me.)

Not only did many of our friends drink a lot, almost all were heavy smokers. Endless cigarettes during the lengthy cocktail hours. Chain smoking at dinner with butts occasionally being snuffed out on used dinner plates. Plus more cigarettes with nightcaps. While I smoked an occasional, solitary cigar and Maisie described herself as a "social smoker"-a pack of Winstons usually lasted her a week-many of her friends who were expecting kept right on puffing away throughout their pregnancies and continued on while they nursed their newborns.

As I look back on those early days, I'm more aware now than I was at the time of what a turbulent period that was for Maisie and me. And for everybody. Even for our friends, who at their many dinner parties feigned ignorance or lack of concern. Shortly after we were married, President Kennedy was assassinated. Cities like Detroit, Chicago—even Philadelphia—were besieged with deadly race riots. Watts, Newark, Berkeley, Jackson, and Montgomery became front-page news. Draft cards were burned in antiwar demonstrations, while it appeared that the war in Vietnam was a lost cause. The secretary of defense called for a nationwide network of bomb shelters. The surgeon general declared that cigarettes caused cancer.

Our friends, however, seemed oblivious to it all and kept on partying and having babies like they were going out of style. All, that is, except Maisie and me.

1964. The cover of Anita's punctually delivered birthday card this year featured a black-and-white photograph of Cassius Clay— mouth and eyes wide open—with the inscription "I am the greatest!" Inside, the card read, "And so are you! Happy Birthday." Anita had written the following note at the bottom of the card: *"Your father says you think Clay's funny / but I don't think that he'll whup Sonny. Happy #27 and many, many more."*

The really big family news that year began to be leaked to me in dribs and drabs (not long after Cassius did whup Sonny). Heather was about to turn twenty-nine and was still looking for a husband. By then she was looking harder than ever because she was worried

she'd become an old maid or that people would think she was a
"lesbo."

I often thought that she intellectually intimidated most of the
guys she dated, and I was sure that she was looking for someone
who was "NOCD," as Mom would describe him: *not our class,
dear*; someone who didn't fit the preppy, WASP, Delafield mold.

This belief that Heather was searching for someone who wasn't
a member of the tribe had been reinforced years before when she
was about to graduate at the top of her class from Vassar (having
completed internships at the Metropolitan Museum of Art and
Christie's). She wrote me at Fort Bragg, saying that she was seeing
a guy by the name of Larry Schwartz who'd been a Whiffenpoof at
Yale and was about to graduate from the School of Architecture. She
said they were kind of engaged—that they hadn't made it official
yet—and that they might get married sometime after Thanksgiving.
I was happy that she'd found the guy she thought she was looking
for, even though her letter made her situation sound a bit tenuous.
She wrote that Dad was thrilled to have another architect in the
family, especially one who had studied at Yale, while Mom was
beside herself with the fact that her only daughter was marrying
a Jew. Unlike my situation with Lisette, Mom couldn't find a way
to hide her embarrassment and encouraged Heather to hold off on
announcing her engagement until she'd graduated. Mom's request
smacked of another war of attrition.

As soon as I received Heather's letter, I phoned her to see how
things were going, a call that was reminiscent of my calls to Lisette
before we were married. Heather's situation was no better than mine
had been: she was paying dearly for having chosen Larry, and our
mother's comments inevitably led to screaming matches between
the two of them. But what made Heather dig her heels in the most
was Mom singing, "stick to your own kind, one of your own kind,"
and then, with considerable sarcasm, adding a tag line from the
Whiffenpoof song: "Lord have mercy on such as we. Baa, baa, baa."

From the tone of our call, I wasn't surprised when two weeks later, I received a telegram from Heather that spared her the embarrassment of another phone call and got her news out of the way as quickly and efficiently as she could. Heather being Heather, she couldn't resist a colorful commentary and used the Vassar code for having a man in your room when telling me what had happened between Larry and her roommate Corrine Davis:

=MOM'S OFF THE HOOK. LAST NIGHT I CAUGHT LARRY SPORTING THE OAK WITH CORRINE AND WE'RE FINISHED. I'M OKAY. BARELY. THEY DON'T MAKE MEN LIKE YOU ANYMORE, FRANNY.
LOTS OF LOVE=
=HEATHER

But in the spring of 1964, things seemed to shift for Heather and her search for a husband. At first all she would tell me was that she'd met a really funny, handsome guy at a friend's wedding who was an unbelievably sexy dancer, but she quickly reminded me that names don't go with stories.

A month or so later, she reported that she'd gone to the Brandywine Raceway with the sexy dancer who had managed the Princeton baseball team and knew all about my pitching career at Episcopal. She added nonchalantly that she'd won a hundred and twenty dollars betting on a trotter named Hanover's Lonely Trey. Two weeks after she'd made a killing at the track, she said that she'd seen a terrific show in New York called *Mame* with the dirty-dancing Princeton guy.

A couple of months passed without any mention of this name-less stranger until Heather invited me to lunch at McGillin's, which by then seemed to have become my private eating club. We'd barely ordered when she poured it all out, clenching her knife and fork in her fists. "Franny, I've got a horrible confession to make, and no, before you ask, I'm not pregnant, although maybe it would be better or make more sense if I was. But I'm not. No, I've fallen in love, seriously in love, with the wrong kind of guy. What makes it worse, he's in love with me, and I think I've got to marry him because I'd never do anything to hurt him. But, here's the rub: he's from the wrong side of the tracks. He's a goddamned Main Line preppy with a fruity first name. It's kind of like Mom handpicked him, and I'm sorry because this isn't the way I wanted it to turn out, and it pisses me off because Mom will think she's won. But she hasn't; Trey has. And I hope I haven't let you down; I just fell head over heels in love with this guy the first time we met, and it's done nothing but get worse—"

I told her to slow down and start from the beginning, with stuff like what this guy's name was and what he did for a living.

Heather said that she was sorry, that she was all mixed up. "His name is Lowell Stockton Rush the Third." She laughed. I thought it was because she was relieved to have gotten what was bothering her out on the table. "A Rush, for God's sake, Franny! A goddamned Rush. How Philadelphia can you get? Trey is his nickname for being 'the Third,' and I almost chucked my cookies when we were introduced, but he immediately knew what I was thinking and said he'd learned to live with it, that it wasn't much worse than being called Lowell or Stocky, and then *he* laughed and said it might grow on me too, and of course I told him somehow I doubted it. What's worse, he went to St. Paul's, Princeton, and Harvard Law and was just made a partner at Ballard, Spahr. You couldn't get any more crème de la crème if you tried, but I love the guy so much, and I can't believe this has happened to me. Of all people."

Well, it did happen to her, even though our mother was furious when Heather and "her beau" resisted announcing their engagement in the society columns for all her friends to see. Mom was even more upset when they slipped away and got married in

Elkton, Maryland. That, of course, caused many of Mom's friends to assume that Heather had eloped because she was pregnant. They were confused, maybe even disappointed, when she didn't have a baby until two years later, but they circulated rumors about her nonetheless.

Unsettling News

On our first anniversary, Maisie said she thought we should take a little inventory to see where we were in our lifelong journey together. Being Maisie, she had every minute of the evening planned, the cornerstone of the celebration being dinner at the Old Guard House Inn in Gladwyne. With Maisie at the helm, the taking of inventory covered lots of ground.

First, we reaffirmed our marriage vows, both swearing that we had no regrets about our choices of life partners, even though Maisie said she didn't think my mother would agree.

"Housekeeping issues" were the next inventory items up for review. Maisie began by saying that we should consider moving to a bigger house as soon as we'd decided to start a family. Next she said that she'd been thinking a lot about how she filled her days, that she could only play so much tennis and get her hair done so many times a month. "So, until we have a baby, I need to do something that's stimulating, maybe even gives me a new identity." She went on to say that she'd thought about taking courses at Penn or Villanova or about getting a job, but one thing kept pushing those ideas out of the way, and she'd made up her mind to become a photographer.

As she had the night we met, she referred to the photographs in *Life* magazine and how she was drawn to them, how she'd like to take pictures that told a story, that captured the soul of her subject.

We both agreed that it was a magical evening, just the way we'd hoped it would be, and the next morning Maisie said that it should become a Delafield family tradition, that we should—no, we must—do "the inventory thing" every anniversary. And, by the end of the week, she'd bought a Pentax camera and all seventeen instructional books from the Life Library of Photography and converted the wash basin area in the basement to a darkroom. It was there that she began her love affair of looking at life through a lens.

Our next anniversary celebration was as reassuring and as much fun as the first. Maisie had discovered that she had an uncanny ability to capture the essence of her subjects in her photographs in varied and unusual ways. She'd even sold a picture of a group of schoolchildren splashing in the fountain in Logan Circle to *The Inquirer*. As a result, her work had become in high demand, and a number of families commissioned her to take pictures of their children. When the evening drew to a close, I raised a glass to her success, but she pooh-poohed my compliments. "All that's fine and dandy, Fran, but I want to do more than just photograph kids. I want some of my own." She smiled and called for the check. "Starting right now."

On our third anniversary, we were guests of Potter and Deirdre's, who, in keeping with our Delafield tradition, took us to the Guard House. The early part of the evening was filled with laughter until Deirdre began to question Maisie about her plans to start a family, saying that she'd better get going, that she was almost thirty. Deirdre's comments hit a raw nerve with Maisie, and she began to sob uncontrollably and couldn't stop. She panicked and waved her hands for everybody to leave her alone, while others in the restaurant stared at her, including a couple of my parents' friends who quickly looked away, perhaps to spare me the embarrassment of being recognized.

The next morning, we sat silently at the island in the middle of our kitchen picking at our breakfasts. Maisie stared through the bay window at her small garden and sipped her coffee as tears began to brighten her eyes and slip down her cheeks. Almost in a whisper, she said, "You know what those friends of your parents at the Guard House were thinking? Saying to each other?"

Before I could answer, she said, "Here's what: that's the Delafield boy, who ran away from college for no good reason, with his home-wrecking slut of a wife."

When I said that I didn't think that was the case, that she was overreacting, Maisie shook her head as though she didn't agree—perhaps in despair—and said, "We're quite a pair, aren't we? Both trying to live down our pasts."

Again before I could speak, she said, "But forget what people think. There's something wrong."

I took a deep breath and squeezed her hand. "We'll see. Give it time."

"But we've been trying for a year." She forced a smile through her tears. "No one can say we haven't given it our best shot."

I said we'd keep on trying. She raised a hand to stop me from saying more. "The time's come. Your mother's started to tell her friends that I'm a barren woman. First she calls me promiscuous, and now barren. I can't win with her. But that's not the point. I've got to get checked out."

I stood and wrapped my arms around her and assured her that no matter what, everything was going to be all right.

Maisie leaned back and kissed me. "That's what I love about you, F. H. Delafield. You're such an optimist. So trusting. But so out to lunch. *So* out to lunch."

In late July, Maisie called me at my office. When I picked up the phone, she hesitated and said that she'd just returned from the doctor's, and then started to cry. "It's not great news."

"Do you want me to come home?" I asked.

She didn't answer.

"Do you?"

She choked out, "No," and then haltingly said, "I'm trying to...to get things...to pull myself together."

For a moment neither of us spoke. Finally, I asked what the problem was.

"Okay, here goes." She hesitated. "All the tests came back negative. Dr. Driscoll says there's no reason why I can't get pregnant. He says I'm fine and we should keep on trying, that many times it takes fifteen months or more. But..."

"But what?"

"It's most probably your problem."

My problem? No way. Things just didn't compute. How could I have gotten Lisette pregnant if I'd had a problem? Had she been pregnant with my child or someone else's? Why did she take Dad's $5,000? Really?

Suddenly I regretted keeping Lisette a secret from Maisie, who continued to cry. "I'm so sorry, Fran, but it doesn't really make any difference whose problem it is, does it? I mean, it's *our* problem, right?"

I said she was right.

"You're sure?"

When I said, "Absolutely," she said that she felt better already.

When I asked if I should get tested, she was slow to answer. "Dr. Driscoll suggests we keep on trying and then, after a year or so, if nothing happens, we should consider adopting."

I said I'd catch the next train—that we needed to explore things further, that we'd see this through together—but Maisie pleaded with me not to come home. "I need some time to myself," she said.

"It's a setback for sure, but it's not as though we've lost a child. We can talk tonight."

"You're sure?"

She said that she'd be okay and once again said that she was sorry. She told me how much she loved me and hung up.

I stared out my office window for a few minutes, registering nothing, until my phone buzzed, jolting me from my trance. I punched the intercom button and told my secretary that I didn't want to take any calls.

"But it's Mr. Morris," Josie said.

I reconsidered and told her to put him through.

"You free for lunch?" Potter asked.

"You're damn right I am."

"My treat," Potter said. "The Philadelphia Club at one?"

"Let's do McGillin's," I said. "I've got some personal stuff to talk about."

I walked to McGillin's oblivious to the midday July heat. My brain was jumbled with half thoughts, and I understood why Maisie had said she was trying to get things together, because I was, too. The truth had suddenly become a burden, a depressing and angering burden. It was no wonder that Lisette had disappeared, no wonder she had taken the money. There was no way she could have been pregnant, and if she was, it wasn't my child; no wonder she wouldn't talk to me when I called La Malbaie. It was all a charade. All that anguish and fighting with my parents for nothing. At that moment, standing outside McGillin's waiting for my old friend who'd been party to most of this, I realized that up until that point, my entire adult life had been determined by Lisette and her lies.

Potter arrived wearing a seersucker suit, button-down shirt, and regimental-stripe bowtie with a white-and-yellow rosette of the City Troop pinned like a miniature fried egg on his lapel. As always he looked squared away, as though the world was his oyster, that he had everything under control. A far cry from my confused life with its many unanswered questions.

We hurriedly settled in, ordered pastrami sandwiches and Cokes, and talked about how bad the Phillies were until our lunches were delivered. "What's up?" Potter finally said. "Something wrong?"

I looked up from my sandwich. "You bet your sweet ass there is."

"Another woman?"

I quickly said, "No," then added, "Well, sort of."

"Spill it, Delafield," he said. "I owe you one."

I told him the whole story, from Lisette's phone call years ago telling me that she was pregnant to Maisie's call within the past hour. I apologized for not telling him all of this years ago, explaining that I'd kept it a secret to protect Lisette and my parents. "Even Maisie doesn't know."

"You're shitting me," Potter said.

I told him that I was going to tell her when I got home.

"Holy shit, Delafield, and I thought marrying Deirdre was the hot Philadelphia gossip."

"And you know what bugs me the most?" I said. "I can still hear Dad saying that Lisette's supposed dilemma was the oldest ploy in the books, that lots of women did it during the war. He told me to offer her five thousand dollars to make it all go away and see what she said then. And when I was at Dartmouth—when I wasn't looking—she took the fucking money and disappeared. Literally disappeared. And I spent the next four and a half years soldiering to pay Dad back. Jesus, Potter, Maisie's right: I'm so fucking out to lunch."

Potter smiled and reached across the table and took my hand. "It cuts two ways, old buddy, so ease up on yourself. The way you trust everyone makes everyone want to trust you. Besides, what's done is done. I'd have been fooled, too."

I fidgeted in my office while I waited for the stock market to close, picking up my phone several times to try to call Lisette, but then quickly hanging up, causing the light for my line to blink on and off at my secretary's desk. After my third or fourth false alarm, Josie knocked on my door, opened it a crack, and asked if I needed something. I waved her away without speaking, but she entered my office and shut the door and asked if everything was okay.

I told her that things were great, that the market was up thirty points.

She made a face that showed that she disapproved of my answer. "Your wife's okay?"

"Better than okay."

"You're sure?" Josie said. "Ever since she called, you've seemed a bit out of sorts."

"Maisie's fine. I promise."

"And Mr. Morris?"

"Potter's great, too. Better than ever."

"Well then, how are *you*?"

"A bit fragile, but everything's going to be fine, thanks, Josie. Just fine. A friend who I thought was a very good friend has really let me down. I've been wrestling with whether or not to call her, but I've decided not to. So, all's okay. I'm sorry to worry you."

Josie smiled. "Promise, Mr. Delafield?" She waited a second for the answer that never came and went back to her desk, quietly closing the door behind her.

I promise, I thought, and pulled open the bottom drawer of my desk, the drawer where I keep my most private papers: Maisie's and my wills, our insurance policies, and our financial statements. I reached to the back of the drawer for a manila envelope marked "Personal," unwound the string that kept it clasped, and pulled two envelopes from it. I brushed some flakes of dried mud from them before setting them on my desk. The first was addressed to Mr. and Mrs. Theodore Delafield at 1212 Poor

Richard's Lane; the second to Lisette Jaud, in care of René Jaud, La Malbaie, Canada.

I studied them for a moment. I felt like I'd never seen them before. They were so unfamiliar, didn't look at all like the letters I remembered writing the night before I was wounded. I placed the letter to Lisette on the corner of my desk and slipped the letter to my parents into the manila envelope and put it back where I had found it.

I reached for the second letter, tapped the edge of the envelope in the palm of my hand, and then tore it in half, and in half again, and in half again, and again, until I couldn't reduce it to anything smaller or less significant and dropped the confetti-like remnants in the wastepaper basket like there was something dirty about them.

As soon as the market closed, I boarded the local commuter train and must confess that I was so intent upon straightening out my jumbled thoughts and angry feelings that I missed my station and rode on to Villanova before I was aware of what I'd done and took a cab back to the Bryn Mawr station to pick up my car.

Maisie was sitting in the kitchen watching the news of the increasingly violent race riots in Newark when I arrived home. She wore a tie-dyed tee shirt over her bathing suit and cradled a Dachshund puppy in her lap. "I can't get up right now," she said. "Oscar Mayer's fallen asleep." A playful smile crossed her face even though her eyes were red and puffy. "I thought we needed something—some living and loving thing—to cheer us up."

At first I thought that getting a puppy at this moment was a bit curious because I'd unsuccessfully lobbied for one a number of times. But I understood how Maisie might find it comforting and thought that she had done it to please me, to take the edge off our dilemma. I lifted the tiny pup from her lap to get a good look at him, held him close to my face and let him lick me, and then brushed my cheek along the puppy's small torso. "Oscar Mayer?"

"Because he looks like a wiener," Maisie said. "The Churchmans had a litter of five and they were ready to go and Oscar wasn't spoken for so...voila! He's just seven weeks, but he's already made me very, very happy. Anyway, Mrs. Churchman said she'd take him back if you don't approve."

I started to say the puppy was just what the doctor ordered but stopped and set him on the floor and pulled Maisie to me. She began to retch with sobs. "It's okay," I whispered. "It's okay. We're going to be fine."

"Oh, Fran, I'm so...so confused and heartbroken...and so sorry."

I told her that she had nothing to be sorry about, that I was the one who should apologize. I switched off the TV and led her to the terrace where I told her every last detail of my deception, from why I'd said I was spoken for when we first met, to the marriage annulment, to the real reason I quit Dartmouth, to Lisette lying to me about being pregnant with my child and what caused my maniacal need to pay my father every cent I owed him. "The irony of it is that I was furious with Lisette for living out her lie until it occurred to me that I've done the exact same thing to you," I said. "So some good may have come from all of this."

Throughout much of our talk, Maisie seemed almost indifferent to what I was saying, so much so that at times I felt as though I was talking to myself. While I'd expected anger and jealousy—even feared that my news, coupled with my inability to be a father, might lead her to ask for a divorce—Maisie was oddly reserved and barely spoke, from time to time crying with me, other times embracing me and occasionally shaking her head in disbelief. At one point she asked, "So this is why you made that weirdo comment at Bar's party that it would be okay with your mother if you got a girl like me pregnant?" I nodded yes and, once again, she retreated into her shell.

When I'd told her everything there was to tell, I said that I felt as though a tremendous weight had been lifted from my shoulders now that all our cards were on the table. I added that for some reason she, too, seemed relieved, almost comforted by all of this. Maisie said that perhaps she was, because now we could start again without any secrets, and she kissed me, saying that all was forgiven, that it really didn't matter who had the problem, that it was ours to solve.

Over time, several of the family members and friends whom Maisie and I took into our confidence speculated that my problem was due to Agent Orange and suggested that I sue the army. The fact that I had left Vietnam before the army started using AO didn't dissuade them one bit. Nonetheless, Maisie and I dealt with the flak and inevitable rumors as best we could, and agreed that if she didn't get pregnant within a year we'd start the adoption process.

1967

Flower Child

One Sunday every month, Maisie and I traveled to Chestnut Hill to have lunch with my parents. Those visits were command performances and over time took on a dulling sameness. They frequently began with Philadelphia snapper soup, then beef and kidney stew, and always included Mom's not-so-subtle, barbed comments followed by pregnant pauses and uneasy glances camouflaged by short-lived smiles. Even though I tried to assure Maisie that our visits were almost as painful for me as they were for her—that they helped keep the family peace, such as it was—she felt that they were a steep price to pay for very little return and had to steel herself for each and every one.

None, however, was more memorable or more painful than our family lunch in late March of 1967, almost exactly nine months after we'd learned that we might have to adopt if we wanted to have a family. While we waited for Heather and Trey to arrive, to avoid talking about where we were in our thinking about adopting— a topic which was of enormous interest to my mother, especially when it came to whose child we would be adopting—I asked Dad if he was going to watch the fight between Muhammad Ali and

Zora Folley on TV. "It may be Ali's last fight," I said, "and your last chance to compare him to Joe Louis."

"There's no comparison," my father said. "Joe Louis never dodged the draft. What's more, he beat that Kraut Schmeling for all of us. I'm just not that interested in Clay, or Ali, or whatever he calls himself."

Even though I knew that Ali's brash statements rubbed Dad the wrong way, I was surprised by his resistance to watch him box because, like so many men of his generation, Dad was an ardent boxing fan. He watched the fights almost every Friday night on Gillette's *Cavalcade of Sports* and reveled at the breakfast table while reading Red Smith's columns about fighters like Willie Pep, Sugar Ray Robinson, and Rocky Marciano. "Do me a favor and watch him," I said. "I think you'll agree you've never seen a heavyweight like him."

My father shook his head. "That's not the issue, Fran. The issue is what kind of a man he is."

I hadn't planned for this to become yet another debate with Dad and forced a smile. "I wasn't talking about his character. I just thought you'd enjoy watching him box."

"But you can't keep character out of this," Dad said. "You, of all people, Fran. You, who fought in Vietnam. You must have some feelings about his refusal to be drafted."

I startled him by saying, "I didn't really go to Vietnam to fight. I was just an unlucky adviser who happened to be in the wrong place at the wrong time."

"But you saved a lot of men's lives," Mom said. "That was fighting, wasn't it?"

"Yes, but, as a result, I helped kill a lot of men, which wasn't something I'd bargained on."

My father drew a Pall Mall from its pack and flipped his Third Army lighter open and shut a couple of times. "Right. Right. I understand. But body counts have always been overstated." He started to light his cigarette but stopped. "And I doubt Vietnam's any different."

"Maybe. Maybe not," I said, "but one body is one too many."

There was a kind look in Dad's eyes as he nodded in agreement. "I can't argue with that."

"But, Theo, Fran was *honoraire*," my mother said. "Those he fought were our enemy."

"Not really," I said. Ali's comment that he didn't have "no quarrel with them Viet Cong" flashed through my mind because when I was in country I didn't have a quarrel with them either. Far from it. When we were recruited to go to Vietnam, we were told that it was nothing more than a civil disturbance that was being fought with pitchforks and ax handles and that we'd be advisers, not combatants. In truth, I'd gone for a change of scene, for an adventure, and never really questioned where it all might lead, certainly never thought that I'd have to kill someone. "Actually, Mom, none of us *really* knew why they were our enemy. It wasn't as simple as your and Dad's war. All we were told was that it had to do with the domino theory. The yellow peril. That it was an attempt to stabilize the region, but that's about it. I doubt many of us thought we were fighting for our country." I paused and looked at Dad. "That's all we knew, and, at the start, it was no different than a training exercise, a war game."

Neither of my parents spoke for a long time. Maisie shifted in her chair. Finally, my father asked, "If you were asked to go back, would you?"

I said of course and then added, "But I wouldn't volunteer to go."

"Are you saying we should have learned our lesson from the French?" my mother asked.

Dad interrupted and said, "Gay, we all know that when it comes to war, the French have very little to teach us."

"*Mon Dieu*," she said. "The lessons are there if you would only listen. America may have different motives than the French but is following the same fruitless path."

Dad shrugged and lit his cigarette. "Fran, I know what you've been through. I really do. Believe me, Son, I experienced much of it after I came home at the end of the war. And I also know that this is a very confusing time for your generation. Don't get me wrong; don't misinterpret my questions. What I'm trying to do is understand."

There was another awkward silence before Maisie said, "Dad Delafield, do you think we should be in Vietnam?"

Dad gave her a quizzical look as though he'd forgotten that she was with us. Later Maisie and I agreed that neither of us had any idea how Dad would answer, and when he said, "No," we both almost fell off our chairs.

"*Vraiment*, Theo?" my mother said. "*Non?*"

"Yes," Dad said. "*Non.*" He took a long drag on his cigarette. "At first I thought we should be there, but that was before I realized it was a war we had no idea how to win. It seems to me that we're winning almost every battle but still losing the war. And one of the things we're losing is a lot of really good kids." He looked at me. "You agree?"

"Yes, sir," I said, "and I lost one of them."

Dad nodded at me, and again the gentle look returned to his eyes. "And you, Maisie?" he asked.

"You know me. I'm the original flower child," Maisie said. "You know, 'make love, not war'?"

My mother flinched at Maisie's comment. "You young people today certainly have minds of your own."

There was another long silence before Heather and Trey entered the living room carrying their six-month-old daughter, Louisa, who immediately became the center of attention.

On our drive home, Maisie said she was sorry and burst into tears. "I'm happy for Heather and Trey with their baby. Really I am. But I'm so unhappy for us, and then…and then…then I had to go and remind your mother of all the stuff she hates about me. And I couldn't tell if your father was pissed at me for putting him on the spot, so I'd write the whole day off as another colossal Maisie fuckup. What was I thinking, talking about making love, not war? Promiscuous Maisie? Home-wrecking queen? Making love, not war. Really! All I want is to put all that behind me and stop always worrying about what people think of me. God, I am such an asshole!"

When I told her that I thought her question was a diplomatic stroke of genius and her peaceful approach to life was one to be admired, she said, "At times, Fran Delafield, you're an asshole, too."

But the following Thursday morning, I was proven right. Josie left a note on my desk saying that my father had called, that he was glad I'd encouraged him to watch the fight, that he thought Ali was remarkable, and that Maisie was remarkable, too—that he admired her courage no end.

Dad's approval surprised and delighted both Maisie and me. What bothered me was that he felt he had to hide his feelings from Mom, in this case delivering them through a "while you were out" note from my secretary.

As always, I wondered why.

Endless Questions

The year of waiting to see if we could start a family had almost passed when major pieces to our puzzle—more accurately, my puzzle—fell into place as things became clearer after Dr. Ames invited me to join him for a week's fishing at the Saint Jean Salmon Club. This apparently innocent excursion began with a flight to Montreal and then on to Gaspé where we spent the night. At dinner, Dr. Ames asked how Maisie was, how we found married life. I told him Maisie was great and that we were handling my problem as best we could. He looked away for a second and mumbled that he was glad to hear it. He paused, took a deliberate sip of his gin and tonic, and said that he wanted to talk to me a little bit more about my health.

I told him that I was in great shape, that I could cast a fly without a hitch, even though I couldn't throw a baseball sixty feet six inches. Dr. Ames shook his head and gave me a fatherly, pay-attention-to-what-I'm-about-to-say look. He said he wasn't talking about my shoulder; he was talking about what I'd referred to as "my problem." He went on to say that he'd known Maisie's gynecologist, Ted Driscoll, for years, and that Dr. Driscoll had taken him into his confidence because so many of his patients had asked him if the reason I couldn't be a father was from my exposure to Agent Orange.

I had no idea where Dr. Ames was headed with this conversation, but after he bent the swizzle stick to his drink until it snapped, I thought I'd put him at ease by telling him that I'd heard all that Agent Orange BS many times before and was used to it by now.

Dr. Ames looked down at the two halves of the swizzle stick and said that both he and Dr. Driscoll agreed with me about Agent Orange. He drew a deep breath and added that they also agreed that I should know the truth. "Fran, Ted's examination and x-rays show conclusively that Maisie is the one who's infertile, that her fallopian tubes are completely blocked. Why, we're never really sure, but it's probably because of endometriosis." His usually kind and understanding eyes were filled with worry, and he repeated a couple of times that he was sorry to have to bear such bad news but thought I had to know.

I was more confused than angry—*dinky dau* all over again, except in Vietnam I had a better idea of who the good guys and the bad guys were—and suddenly I didn't know whom to believe, whom to trust, and all of those in question were people I loved and who said they loved me too. I couldn't make sense out of any of it. Not a bit. I just sat in that funky little French-Canadian restaurant a thousand miles from home and stared at a man whom I'd always viewed not only as a family friend but as a friend of mine, a man who professed to be giving me the greatest gift of all: the truth, even though in giving it, he'd turned my life upside down.

When I finally calmed myself enough to speak, I asked if Dr. Driscoll had told Maisie what Dr. Ames had just told me. He said he had. "Not only that, Ted reviewed her case with a specialist at Pennsylvania Hospital and followed up with a phone call to her."

I asked if Dr. Ames was sure about all of this.

"Yes, I'm sure, but I'm not surprised," he said. "It's not uncommon, Fran. Endometriosis has the nasty habit of seeking out intelligent, well-educated women like Maisie. Things would have been different if you'd had your sperm count checked, but Maisie rejected that idea. Ted said she kind of panicked when he suggested it. That's why he finally talked with me. He thought you would accept this better coming from me rather than from Maisie and hoped that eventually both of you would talk with him about your dilemma."

It was then that I asked the unanswerable: Why would Maisie lie to me? Place the blame on me?

Dr. Ames shook his head, looked down at his untouched dinner, and said he had no idea. None whatsoever. He said it was between Maisie and me, but that Dr. Driscoll had assured him that it wasn't the first time one of his patients had done something like this.

Small consolation, I thought.

From that point on, we picked at our food without speaking. Before dessert Dr. Ames interrupted the silence and listed the names of the men who would be fishing with us. He said that I had met many of them the weekend I'd caught my great fish and added that there would be a surprise guest whom he hoped would cheer me. M. Trudeau and René were the only people I could think of, but I was so preoccupied with the news about Maisie that I went right back to trying to make sense of what Dr. Ames had just told me.

Later, outside our hotel rooms, both of us fidgeting with our room keys, Dr. Ames again said he was sorry to have to deliver such confusing news. As we shook hands good night, he said, "Believe me, Fran, Ted and I agonized over telling you this. I hope I've done the right thing—medical ethics be damned."

I assured him that he had, even though I wasn't any more sure of what I'd said than I was about anything else I'd learned that night.

We arrived at the St. Jean Salmon Club with just enough time to unpack before lunch. When we entered the dining cabin, a few of the other fishermen had already gathered for drinks. Dr. Ames reintroduced me, asking with a laugh if anyone remembered his young friend whose first salmon was thirty-seven pounds. They all shook their heads in mock disbelief, and more than one asked, "How in the hell will we ever forget him, Bill?"

Once the introductions were complete, the conversation was filled with questions about late June / early July fishing on other salmon rivers, mostly the Restigouche, the Grand Cascapedia, and the Big Laxa. Just before the dinner bell was rung, M. Trudeau entered as though he was the host and in charge of everyone present. He was followed by René, who carried Boom Boom in one hand and a violet beret in the other.

M. Trudeau worked his way to me and greeted me warmly, saying he hoped that we would have some time alone to discuss some *ancien histoire.* He smiled a knowing smile. "In particular your brief stay with me and your friend Potter's mysterious rationale for leaving La Malbaie and dragging you away with him. I would have welcomed it if you had stayed, but we will talk."

Yet another surprise, and I flinched at his comment. I remembered Potter telling me that it was his father's deal with M. Trudeau and that it included both of us. And now I was being told that I could have stayed and wondered what that would have meant. For me. For Lisette. For a whole list of things. All I could think was that this was turning out to be one hell of a trip, when René greeted me with an awkward hug, pressing Boom Boom between us, and hurriedly saying that it had already been agreed that we would fish together that afternoon.

My heart sank with disappointment that René was my surprise, although I didn't know whom I'd actually expected, even though after my discussion with Dr. Ames the night before, I'd fantasized that Lisette might appear. I also wondered who'd already decided that I would fish with René: Dr. Ames. M. Trudeau? Max nix to me, I thought, and made up my mind that I would put the time with René to good use, to try to get some answers to my many questions about Lisette.

Apparently, René had the same thought, and after lunch he suggested that we get some fresh air. He picked up his nervous little dog, and he and I walked to a bench that overlooked the river's Home Pool, where we sat and watched a small salmon jump a few times. René dismissed the fish's antics with a *pfiff*, saying that the river was too low for good fishing. Then, in the same casual tone, he said that Lisette was living and working in La Malbaie and hoped she could come see me.

I was confused and filled with a sense of guilt, or if it wasn't guilt, some feeling that made me very, very uneasy, and I began asking René questions without giving him time to answer.

Why now?

After all these years?

Why not when I returned from Vietnam?

When I'd tried so hard to reach her?

When I'd talked to her on the phone?

And what happened to the baby?

René said all that was between the two of us—exactly what Dr. Ames had said when I asked him why Maisie would lie to me.

When René asked if it would be all right if Lisette visited the next day, for some reason I hesitated before answering. I guess I was having trouble adjusting to yet another change, another issue that could change the way I imagined the truth—and what it all meant for Maisie and me. When I said yes, I'd welcome her, René was pleased and without any more discussion said that we should be ready to start fishing at four thirty and clucked at Boom Boom to follow him back to his cabin.

After René left, I sat and studied the river, wondering what secrets lay beneath its broken surface and if it was trying to tell me something—perhaps that, like its currents, the truth was frequently disguised and difficult to discover. Random thoughts ran through my mind. I was thirty years old, had been happily married for four years—or, until the night before, I thought Maisie and I had been happy and honest with each other. Now, all of a sudden, I was about to be with a woman I hadn't seen or talked to for almost twelve years, a woman who for a little more than a month had been my wife. I tried to convince myself that a visit from Lisette was a good thing, a necessary thing, that I might finally know the truth and close that chapter of my life, as she had closed it years before, once and for all.

Finally, the Truth

The next day, after the bell had clanged for lunch and the last of the fishermen had disappeared into the dining cabin, I stood on the lawn at a loss for what to do, wondering if there was an affliction that combined both physical and emotional paralysis. Time seemed to stand still until Lisette emerged from the kitchen, followed by a girl with a head full of knotty blond curls. As Lisette started down the steep wooden stairs toward me, I found it hard to draw a full breath. She was still the most beautiful woman I'd ever known, except now she carried herself with confidence. Clearly she wasn't the shy teenager whom I'd married. But, as she stepped onto the grass and walked to me, she looked more petite than I remembered. She smiled and gave me a short wave, and all I could think was goddamn everybody and everything for robbing me of this woman's love.

For quite a while, we stood together without as much as a greeting. Holding each other said all that needed to be said. It confirmed the pain of our separation and the joy of being reunited. Soon I could feel her begin to sob while she pressed against me, and I was surprised by how frail she felt.

When we separated, Lisette took the young girl's hand and gently pulled her toward us. The girl looked up and smiled with

Lisette's hesitant smile, and I didn't need to be told who she was. Suddenly the magnitude of this meeting simply overwhelmed me: this adorable girl was our daughter. My daughter. I wanted to take her in my arms and hold her forever, but, instead, I stuffed my hands in my pockets and shook my head in disbelief.

In happiness.

In approval.

Lisette said that the girl's name was Francine, that she was eleven, and that she had wanted her daughter to meet her dear friend from the United States who spoke such beautiful French and years ago had caught a great salmon.

Francine curtseyed before shaking my hand. We spoke in English, and then in French for her mother's sake, as we wandered to the river and sat on the bench that overlooked the Home Pool. As we talked, I was reminded of our first night together in M. Trudeau's convertible when we'd asked questions a mile a minute and answered all with great enthusiasm. More than once our first kiss ran through my mind, and I looked at Lisette to see if she sensed what I was thinking, but she seemed oblivious to it all and told Francine that her *grand-oncle* was waiting for her, that René had planned a special surprise for her and said she should take her bathing suit with her.

After Francine left us, we walked farther downriver to a grassy spot at the water's edge and sat close to each other and watched and listened as the river slipped past us, its glassy, green water sparkling in the midday sun. Oddly, our rapid-fire conversation stopped as quickly as it had begun. For a while—for a period that eventually became uncomfortably long for me—neither of us spoke, although at one point Lisette touched my arm to get my attention but then shook her head and pulled her knees to her chest, wrapped her arms around them, and laid her head on her arms. Her eyes had begun to tear even though she was smiling, and, without my asking, she said yes, Francine was our child.

I was elated. My trust in Lisette had been well founded and, more importantly, restored. And even though her comment raised more questions—not only about Lisette and Francine and me, but about Maisie and me—it helped me get closer to the truth, although what I learned was irrelevant, for none of it could be reversed or relived, but it did help me better understand what had happened while I was at Dartmouth: Lisette's inability to speak English contributed to her feeling of isolation, and only once did she and my mother have a meaningful conversation. The rest of the time, Mom spoke at her, or around her, in English. And, while Dad struggled with his pidgin French, Lisette said that my mother's disdain for her was *tangible*, and on most occasions Lisette would excuse herself and go to our empty room and cry and cry, and cry some more.

When she had her one momentous conversation with Mom, it was far different from what she'd described in her farewell letter. Yes, my mother was concerned about us being too young and that Lisette didn't speak English, but the comments that convinced her that our situation was hopeless, that we'd made a terrible mistake, came when Lisette mustered the courage to tell her about her grandfather.

My mother called it "the straw that broke the camel's back." She said that the Peltiers and Delafields could never be accused of having "a touch of the tar brush," that Lisette must leave immediately, and promised not to tell my father if she went away quietly because if he ever found out, he would disown me for shaming the Delafield name. Mom told Lisette that it was as though I had purposefully set out to insult my parents, and I couldn't have done a better job of it if I'd tried. She ended the conversation by asking Lisette if she could imagine what an insult it would be for their first grandchild—traditionally a source of great joy and celebration—to be both a Catholic *and* part Negro.

And that night, without a question or a comment, Dad wrote a check for $5,000 to send her on her way. The next day, after he'd helped her load her suitcase on the train, they stood in the space between the cars, and he put out his hand and said *au revoir*. For some reason, and Lisette still wasn't sure why, she slipped inside his hand and embraced him, and he held her tight, kissed her on the forehead, and took her hands in his. When she looked up at him, she thought he was crying. In very bad French, he called her his *bru*—his daughter-in-law—and wished her well and said he knew I loved her very, very much.

Lisette had cried at my father's words and was crying while she told me this. I wrapped my arm around her shoulders and pulled her to me to comfort her, and, after a moment, she kissed me, at first her lips barely touching mine.

Later, as we lay together in my small cabin, I asked, why now? Why not when we talked on the phone when I had called to locate René?

"Because your mother was right," she said. "Our life together would not have worked. We never would have found peace and happiness, and I wouldn't have been strong enough to lose you a second time."

"But—"

"I know, Fran, but that is what I thought. What I believed. I have revisited that decision every day since your call, and my life has been filled with regrets."

"Mine too, because you were wrong," I said. "We would have found a way. You have to understand that I loved you then and love you now."

"So why now? Because it is important that you finally know the truth." She paused. "Because it might be the last time you will ever see me. I am sick with the same cancer that took my mother, and I wanted you to meet Francine."

When I tried to say something, she pressed her finger against my lips. "So you see, my prophet, I have kept my word. I have never loved another man and never will. I will die with you as my husband, for I burned the annulment papers that you signed. It was a symbol of my love for you, and I wondered what harm it would do because we were never to see one another again. But things have changed, and I wanted you to meet our child because someday soon she will need you."

She lifted her finger from my lips and asked if I was angry with her. I found myself overwhelmed with regret, with sadness and, oddly, with joy.

Regret that I hadn't pursued her one more last, desperate time.

Sadness for her and her child—and, yes, for myself—that she was dying.

And joy because I never knew that anyone would care that deeply for me.

"Does Francine know all of this?" I asked.

She said no but that she would tell her in time, and I promised that I would look after her when the time came that she needed me.

Maisie's Dilemma

I had no idea how to approach Maisie about her infertility or to tell her about Lisette and Francine and was confused by the fact that technically I was a bigamist. Technically, hell; I was married to two women, was in love with both of them, and never dreamed that such a thing was possible.

The minute I got home, before I could begin to address any of these issues, Maisie said that she had bad news for me: Potter had been let go by SK&F and wanted to talk with me as soon as possible. I thought it would be best to get Potter's problem out of the way—and give me some breathing room to clear the decks before confronting Maisie—so I called him. At first we talked in our familiar prep school code, skillfully avoiding the central issue, until I couldn't wait any longer and asked what the hell happened at SK&F. In a matter-of-fact fashion, Potter said it was pretty simple, that he should have seen it coming. "Apparently we had a lot of business failures that I wasn't aware of, and we are—correct that, Delafield—*they are* about to lose patent protection on one of their biggest-selling drugs."

I was surprised to hear him laugh, and even more surprised that it sounded like an honest-to-God, something-was-tickling-his-funny-bone laugh. "It's kind of comical," he said. "I mean here they are, 'the fine old house of the pharmaceutical industry,' and they're selling sunglasses and suntan lotion and cosmetics that look like dildos—all of this to fend off the inevitable."

I said I was surprised, that he sounded relieved.

"Actually, Delafield, I am. If it hadn't been for my old man, I'd have quit long ago. Big business just isn't my bag. No matter—it's been a huge shock to him, and he kept asking if I'd screwed up somehow. It never occurred to me that it would hurt him—worse, make him feel that I'd let him down. But when he called his friends at the company to see if things couldn't be straightened out, most of them had been fired, too. It's as though the muckety-mucks went through the stud book and got rid of everybody, including a bunch of family members. You can bet they'll be talking about this at the Rabbit and the Philadelphia Club for years."

"So you're okay?" I asked.

Potter assured me that he was, and from his tone I believed him. When I asked what he thought he'd do next, he said he hoped to find a teaching job where he could coach racquet sports, that it was something he'd always wanted to do. "So, Delafield," he said, "whenever you think that your life's been fucked up, just think of me." As we hung up, I thought that if Potter only knew…if only he knew the truth, he wouldn't think he had a corner on a fucked-up life.

By the time I'd finished talking with Potter, Maisie was sipping a gin and tonic and arranging supper and a pitcher of iced tea on a tray. When she asked how Potter was, I said I thought he'd be fine, that we could talk about him later, that we had to talk. I followed her to the terrace where she set the tray on the table and lowered her head as if she were meditating. "You've got a problem. Right?"

Her question caught me off guard, and, as I helped her set the plates and glasses at their places as though their order was foremost on my mind, I asked what made her say such a thing. "Chalk it up to a woman's intuition," she said and paused. "You saw that Canadian girl when you were fishing, didn't you?"

"What makes you think—?"

"What else could it be?" she asked.

"It's more complicated than that," I said. "Lots more."

I began by telling her about my conversation with Dr. Ames. When she tried to explain, I interrupted her, asking that she hear the full story first. But she said she didn't give a damn about the full story, that she wanted her day in court, and between sobs she said that I couldn't possibly understand what she'd been going through. Not possibly. "When you can't have kids, it seems like everyone else is having them, and it's horrible. Just horrible. You have no idea how painful that is, Fran. No idea."

When I tried to tell her that I understood, she dismissed me with a wave of her hand. "And you think you've got a story? Well, here's mine. All throughout our marriage, we've been pretty good at sweeping lots of stuff under the rug, but it may come as a surprise to you that I think about my reputation of being a home wrecker almost every day. I'm still so embarrassed by what I did, even though there's nothing I can do about it, nothing at all, except be faithful to you and be the kind of wife you'd be proud of. Over the years these feelings boiled up less and less frequently until it became known that we were having trouble getting pregnant. I imagined your mother, and lots of others, saying, 'First he goes and marries that home-wrecking slut, and then it turns out she's barren.' Do you understand, Fran?"

I said I did.

She shook her head. "I doubt it. I was scared. Scared to death and embarrassed and ashamed, and I chickened out. It was a horrible, dishonest thing to do, and you'll never know how sorry I am, but I couldn't face the accusations and more embarrassment and thought it really didn't matter which one of us had the problem because it was *our* problem, that either way we'd have to adopt if we wanted kids."

She stood and looked down at me. "Okay? Is that what you wanted to know? Wanted to hear?" She grabbed her plate, raised it above her head, and smashed it on the flagstones. "Is it?" She threw her glass, shattering it as well. "You happy now? Feel better that it's my problem, not yours? That your reputation is intact and mine, once again, is in the sewer?"

I reached for her arm and was surprised when she didn't pull away but merely shook her head and muttered, "God, I hate myself. Hate myself. I'm such an asshole!"

I stood and took her in my arms to comfort her.

"I'm sorry, Fran," she said, over and over. "I'm ashamed of what I did to you. Because you're so trusting, it was like taking candy from a baby. It was too easy to be right. Can you ever forgive me?"

Up until that point, the anger and resentment that I'd felt about her lying to me had been overwhelming and in my darkest moments had caused me to wonder if social inertia had predestined me to marry a woman of Maisie's background. Had I overlooked her reputation as a promiscuous home wrecker simply because on paper she had all the proper boxes checked? Was she no more than a matter of social convenience? These questions haunted me once I'd learned of her lie, but at that moment, I understood what Maisie had been going through and told her so, and said she was forgiven. Forever.

"We'll see," she said, "but I wouldn't blame you if you threw me out on the street where I belong."

She eased from me and began picking up the pieces of her plate. Again I took her arm and gently set her back in her chair. She seemed to accept everything I did without resisting. It was as though she'd surrendered. "Take a deep breath and believe me when I say you're forgiven, because I mean it," I said. "And try to forgive *me*, because it doesn't end there. You're right about my seeing Lisette. René arranged a surprise meeting with her. It was the first time I'd seen or talked to her since she left me and went back to Canada, and that's the God's truth."

I paused and asked Maisie if she was okay. If she was ready for what came next. She pressed her hands flat against her cheeks but nodded for me to continue. "Okay, here goes." I placed my hands over hers to connect with her. "I'm the father of an eleven-year-old girl. She was with Lisette, and her name is Francine."

Maisie freed her hands from mine and ran them back over her hair. "You've got to be kidding, Fran. How much worse can it get?"

"Worse than you can imagine. To start, Lisette never had our marriage annulled, so right now I'm married to you both."

Maisie sat upright. In an instant her demeanor changed as though a switch had been thrown. "What do you mean you're married to us both?" Before I could answer, she said, "Well, that won't last for long, Fran, because it's either her or me. First love, first broken heart, first fuck versus barren, home-wrecking slut. A no-brainer if there ever was one, especially now that you've discovered a child of your own."

"That's not the way I see it."

"Well, you're wrong—"

I raised my hands, trying to silence her. "Here's the worst part, the most important part of all." Perhaps it was my tone of voice, but for some reason Maisie settled back in her chair as though she was ready to hear me out.

When I told her that Lisette had terminal cancer, she whispered, "Oh, my God. I can't believe this is happening. What does that mean?"

"I don't know," I said. "I don't even know how much time she's got. A few months? A year? I just don't know."

Maisie muttered, "Oh, my God," again and turned away from me. "Timing's not the real issue," she said. "What about the girl? What happens to her when...when her mother dies?"

"She's my daughter. You know, my responsibility."

"I know, only too well," Maisie said. "I can't compete with that or with a woman who gave you a child—something I'll never be able to do—a child who will be a constant reminder of her mother and what a failure I am." She collected my plate and silverware and set them on the tray.

I said that I didn't think we'd quite finished, and she looked down at me, the tray trembling in her hands. "Wrong. I'm finished. I'm cleaning up." Tears ran down her cheeks. "And then I think I'll take Oscar Mayer for a little walk. I need to be alone for a while."

I reached for her and asked how I could help. She stepped away from me. "Nothing you can do will help."

After she returned from her walk, Maisie said she wanted to be alone and shut herself in the bedroom. Thunder clouds darkened the evening sky, and the stifling July heat and humidity was quickly replaced by prolonged gusts of wind and a sudden drop in temperature, and then by thunder and lightning. Eventually the storm knocked out our electricity, and while I lit a few candles, Maisie retrieved Oscar from the refuge of his crate and sat silently comforting him in her lap, staring at the rain as darkness surrounded us.

I asked if she wanted to talk, and she said that she guessed she did, and then added that there wasn't much else to say. When I asked how she felt about Francine, she said she didn't want to have anything to do with her, that I was right; she was my responsibility. "Besides, there's no way to explain her." With that, she picked up one of the candles and said she was going to bed and was taking Oscar with her.

As she walked from the kitchen, the flickering light from her candle threw an ominous shadow on the cabinets behind her. At that moment I thought everything in our lives was cloaked in shadows, that nothing was clear or easy to see. Although I wanted to stop her, to tell her again that I needed her now more than ever and that all was forgiven, I didn't think she wanted to hear any of that, I and wished her a good night's sleep, saying that hopefully things would look different in the morning.

Une Larme

An unusually hot and humid two weeks dragged by with very little communication between Maisie and me. When we did speak, we never came anywhere near resolving the issues facing us. We just went over and over old ground until we were tired and frustrated by our discussions and left things drifting and contentious.

Then, the last week in July, Maisie left to visit her parents in their Watch Hill summer home for two weeks, leaving me alone for the first time since we'd been married. In an odd way, I welcomed it, hoping that it would give me the opportunity to put things into perspective, that the time apart would soften Maisie's attitude and make her more open to accepting Francine, something that seemed to become more and more imminent with each phone call to Lisette.

When Maisie returned home, she greeted me with a wave and a weak smile but was even chillier and more distant than before she'd left, and my hopes that her attitude might have changed quickly disappeared. Moreover, she wasn't her usual scrubbed, energetic-looking self; she was haggard, her hair matted and drawn tight in a ponytail. While she spread her clothes across our bed and piled some on the floor, I tried to show interest in her time in Rhode Island, but she barely spoke to me, seemingly concentrating on a blouse that she folded and refolded several times. Finally, she turned to me and said, "Fran, I don't think you get it. I'm not unpacking. I'm packing."

"Oh?" I said, trying to remain calm. "Where are you going this time?"

"Home."

"But this is your home."

She shook her head. "Your home maybe, but not mine. Not now. I'm going home to live with my mom."

"*Live* with or *stay* with?"

"Live with. I can't stay here any longer. Can't stand our fishbowl lives."

At that point I asked what the hell had happened in Watch Hill.

"Nothing. Nothing at all, except it gave me time to think."

"Well, you got it all wrong," I said. "First of all, I still love you. Secondly, you don't have anything to run away from here that we can't handle together. I want you to stay."

"Wow," she said. "You're so naïve. Once you've decided what to do about your daughter, the damning judgments will come pouring out of the woodwork. It would be hell around here for me. An absolute nightmare, and I'm not willing to suffer another one."

"Forget about what other people think," I said, "especially if you care about me."

"You? You mean you and your daughter." She threw the blouse she'd been folding into her suitcase. "Not right now. Right now all I care about is taking care of Maisie. Maybe someday I'll worry about us again, but not now, Fran. Not right now."

All the rest—the tears, the finger pointing, the "yes, buts," the forced apologies, and the pleading—accomplished nothing, and the next day Maisie took Oscar Mayer and drove to Greenwich, leaving me alone to try to find a solution to our dilemma and wait for the inevitable news from La Malbaie.

———— ∞ ————

Early the week following Labor Day, my secretary buzzed me. A Mr. Jaud was on the line. I grabbed for the phone, knowing that this was the call that I'd dreaded. René said that Lisette had taken a turn for the worse and did little else but talk of how much she would like to see me. When I asked how much time she had, René answered, "You should be here today."

I have no memory of the flights to Quebec City or the drive to La Malbaie because I was preoccupied with whether or not Lisette would live long enough to see me. It was close to dark when I arrived at M. Trudeau's summer house, where René waited for me in the familiar Mercedes convertible. As I pulled next to him, René hurried from his car, momentarily juggling Boom Boom in his arms before setting him on the gravel drive. He said Lisette was hanging on to see me once more and added, "It's good you came today. We should not waste any time."

A few minutes later, we parked in front of a bungalow nestled in a cluster of small, look-alike, one-story houses. A single light shone above its front stoop where René paused and nervously stroked Boom Boom's head. "There is something I would like to say, something you should know, Fran. When Lisette was diagnosed with cancer, her doctor told her that she should prepare for the worst. Frankly, I had great trouble with the doctor's *froideur*, but it may have been a blessing because it forced her to prepare Francine for what almost certainly lay ahead." In the dim porch light, his eyes were glistening. "Excuse me," he said in French, wiping at his tears. "When I learned how sick she was, I blamed myself for keeping you apart. I broke my covenant with you, my promise to be a real friend."

I finally understood how hard this had been for René and tried to relieve his guilt as best as I could. "You only did what Lisette wanted."

René sniffled and cleared his throat. "Yes and no. If only I'd let you reach her just once—just one more time, Fran, just one more time—perhaps you would have reunited."

When I reminded him that I'd tried to talk with her when I called La Malbaie but that she'd refused, René seemed to relax for a moment, only to lapse quickly back into his self-incrimination. "It's not your fault, René," I said. "It's really not. For some reason, beyond you and me, it wasn't meant to be."

He nodded and reached to open the door, then placed a hand gently to my chest to slow me. "*En garde*, Fran. This isn't the beautiful Lisette…" He hesitated. "The beautiful Lisette you knew as a young woman, not even the frail beauty you saw this summer. Her disease has done its cruel damage." Again he reached to open the door and added, "The nurse is Sister Claire."

We entered without knocking and stood in the low-ceilinged hallway where we could see into the bedroom. Francine sat on the edge of the bed with her back to us, her head bowed. A woman in a pale-blue-and-white nun's habit was leaning over the figure in the bed and appeared to be repeating whatever it was she was saying. René nodded, and we walked to the bedroom doorway. Sister Claire looked up and told Lisette that she had visitors.

Lisette stared at the ceiling and almost inaudibly asked who was visiting her.

Francine turned and told her mother that it was Uncle René and that he'd brought her a happy surprise.

Lisette took a labored breath, but her expression didn't change. It seemed that speaking or looking about her was a struggle. "*Une surprise?*"

Francine stood and walked around the bed, ran a hand down René's arm, and smiled at him much in the same shy manner her mother would have. But I had no idea what to expect, had no idea how Francine would handle all of this. At eleven, she was about to lose her mother—up until recently her only parent—and would be left alone to be taken in by her elderly bachelor uncle or by me, a total stranger.

What happened next surprised me, thrilled me, and complicated my life forever. Francine opened her arms, inviting me to embrace her. I hesitated and then pulled her to me. She was so small and delicate that I was afraid I'd crush her, but the clinging, desperate nature of her hug made me think that she was seeking strength and stability from me, and I held her tight, the top of her curly blond head barely reaching my breastbone. She looked up at me and said that my being there would make her mother very happy. "Thank you for coming, Papa," she said, as though she'd known all along that I was her father and that I would be there when she needed me, as though Lisette had been preparing her for this moment since the day she was born.

Francine let go of me and gently turned her mother's head in my direction and told her that I was René's surprise. Lisette moved a bruised hand toward me and smiled for a second, her pale lips drawing tight across her now prominent teeth. I took her hand, not really sure if she knew who I was until she whispered, "*Mon prophète.*"

I stroked her cheek and was shocked by how cool it was. I said that I'd come to tell her how much I loved her, to assure her that I would take the best of care of Francine. And I kissed her.

For a moment she didn't speak. With great effort she said, "Thank you," and weakly squeezed my hand. "Now, will you light a candle for me so I can see where I am going?"

Sister Claire handed me the unlit candle from the bedside table and fished a pack of matches from the table's narrow drawer. I lit the candle so Lisette could see it and placed it back on the table. *Une larme*—a single, crystal tear—rested on each of her cheeks. Her smile returned, and she turned her head slowly toward Sister Claire and in a hoarse whisper said, "I am ready now."

The sister told her that God was preparing a place for her and then looked at me and said she was afraid that the time had come for only family to be present. René spoke very quietly, saying that I must stay. When Sister Claire asked who I was, I interrupted and told her that I was Lisette's husband.

Sister Claire flinched. "Impossible."

René assured her that it was the truth. She shook her head in amazement and asked Francine if I really was her papa. Again the sister looked taken aback when Francine nodded and pointed to the wedding band on Lisette's boney hand and said, "She asked me to put it on her this morning, to complete the circle."

At first Sister Claire gave me a rather long, cold look and then muttered, "My God! Surprise after surprise," and apologized and welcomed me.

Our vigil with Lisette lasted longer than any of us would have predicted, and I was reminded of my experience in Vietnam and how, for whatever reason, I had fought so hard to beat the odds even though the doctors thought I was a goner for sure. I was amazed how strong the human will was, how badly we all want to hang on to this thing we call life, as imperfect as it may be. And now here was this frail woman whom I had fought to live for, racked with pain while fighting to fend off the inevitable. I thought this was one of the many things we had in common, one of the many things we never had, and never would have, a chance to share.

René invited me to spend the night at his house, but I declined. He excused himself, saying that he would be back first thing in the morning. Near midnight Sister Claire convinced Francine to go to bed and showed me to the couch where I could sleep while she made herself comfortable in a small easy chair by Lisette's bed.

I wrestled with sleep for a while and then tiptoed back to Lisette's bedside. The room was lit only by a floor lamp. The candle on the bedside table by then had burned out, and Sister Claire slept heavily in her chair, a blanket pulled to her chin. I stood for a long time staring at Lisette, trying to imagine how beautiful she had been when we first met, when we were so in love. She seemed to be at peace, and I lay next to her and rested my arm gently across her chest and whispered that I hoped somehow she could hear me, that I wanted her to know how much I loved her. And always would.

I lay with her for close to an hour, but when she gave a faint kick under the covers, I sat and looked down at her. The soft sound of her breathing had stopped. I waited a moment before waking Sister Claire and then went to wake my daughter and tell her that her mother was gone and to comfort her in any way I could, except it was Francine who comforted me.

Difficult Decisions

With help from René and Sister Claire, I busied myself with the logistics around the undertaker and the service, in part to avoid the other issues that faced me: Did I move to La Malbaie? Or have Francine live with Lisette's sister, who had married and moved to Saskatchewan? Or have her live with René? Or did I take her home, and if so, would Maisie be there to mother her?

On the Maisie question, there was only one way to find out the answer. I called Greenwich, worried that the call might be as unsuccessful as my many earlier attempts in which Maisie had refused to talk with me. On each call I was consoled by her mother, who urged me to be patient, assuring me that things would right themselves and that we would be back together soon. "I went through one of these difficult times with Maisie years ago," her mother had said, "and she proved to be amazingly resilient. So don't give up hope, Fran. I think she processes pain more openly, but maybe a little more slowly, than most."

When Mrs. Bingham answered the phone, she asked if I could call a little later, saying that Maisie was still asleep, and she didn't think she was quite ready to talk. When I told her that I had to speak with Maisie right away, her mother said that I sounded upset and asked if everything was okay.

I said no, everything wasn't okay, that everything was pretty much a mess. I was tempted to describe my situation but stopped and asked if Maisie had told her about Canada. Her mother hesitated long enough that I knew the answer. "It's okay if she has," I said. "We're all trying to get to the truth right now. To do what's best."

Mrs. Bingham cleared her throat. "I think she's told me everything—everything about her infertility and about your situation in Canada. It's all so unbelievable, and I'd like to help in any way I can."

"Well then, please wake her and tell her that Lisette has died and that I want her to come home, that my daughter is going to need a mom, and I need her, too."

Maisie sounded sleepy and distracted when she said hello.

"It's good to hear your voice," I said.

"I'm sorry about Lisette."

I told her that it had happened faster than I'd expected and that Francine would be coming home with me in a few days.

"Thanks for letting me know. You were good to call," Maisie said, sounding as though she was about to hang up.

The adrenaline surge caught me by surprise. "I was good to call? What kind of comment is that? You're my wife, for Christ's sake, Maisie. The woman I've made a life with, the woman of my future, and I need you. And Francine's going to need you too, more than she's going to need me. Get it? We can't do this without you, and I want you by my side."

Maisie tried to interrupt, but I wouldn't let her. "But you don't get it, do you? I love you. I really do, and I need your friendship, and sometime soon you're going to need mine, too. I'm your strongest ally, and we'll work through all this crap together. And, if you need to hear it again, you're forgiven and there's no need to try to run away from anything because none of it makes a damn bit of difference to me. Besides, you'll never really find a place to hide. So, please, come home, Maisie. I need you and want you now more than ever."

"Wow, Fran, I've never heard you talk like that," she said and asked that I give her a little more time. I could hear her mother saying that she processed pain more slowly than most but was amazingly resilient and decided to honor Maisie's request. I also thought I'd like to let Reverend Crawford know that I was learning how to give an intentional pass.

My father had barely picked up the phone when he asked where I was. In a somewhat scolding tone, he said that he'd been trying to reach me for days, that no one had answered my home phone and my secretary had said that I was in Canada but didn't know how to get in touch with me or when I'd be returning. He paused, a pause that gave me a minute to decide how much of my situation to tell him. He interrupted my thoughts by saying, "Your mother's not doing well. She's been bedridden for the last few days, and the doctors say if things don't begin to look up soon, she'll have to go to the hospital. She'd appreciate a visit from you, and so would I."

I apologized for being so hard to reach and said I was sorry that Mom was sick and that I'd be home in a few days. Dad's voice rose over the phone. "In a few days? What are you doing in Canada anyway?"

"Dad, I've got a few problems of my own," I said. "I'll come see you and Mom just as soon as I can, but Lisette died last night, and I'm going to stay for her funeral."

Dad's tone softened immediately, and he said how sorry he was and asked what had happened.

I told him it was a long story, that I'd explain everything when I got home. "So, tell Mom I hope she feels better and that I'll see her in a few days. And be strong, Dad. I'll be there just as soon as I can."

"Got it," he said and surprised me by saying, "If it weren't for your mother's situation, I'd be there with you for Lisette's service. I know how much she meant to you."

Other surprising things happened as I finalized the funeral arrangements. All were positive, and all somewhat overwhelming.

First, M. Trudeau invited me to bury Lisette in his family plot as a gift to recognize what he called "a truly moving story of young love."

Second, I was surprised when René handed me his suggestion for the wording on Lisette's headstone: "Lisette Jaud Delafield. 1937–1967. Loyal wife, mother, and family friend." It wasn't the sentiment that shook me; it was the fact that René suggested that Lisette be remembered as a member of the Delafield family—not the Jaud family—for eternity.

And last, but far from least, Heather came to the funeral, and with her came letters from Trey and Potter. I couldn't believe that they all knew how much this would mean to me. Moreover, Francine seemed to fall in love with Heather instantly, going back and forth between French and English, even giggling a great deal, over what I would never know, except more than once Francine said that my sister was "a silly."

But, of course, "a silly" is the last thing Heather is. She was the one who suggested that she and René be with me when I talked to Francine about her future and the difficult choices she had to make. When we finally found a quiet moment the afternoon before Lisette's service, we huddled in Francine's small bedroom to talk with her. I stood with my back to the door while Heather and Francine stretched out on the bed leaning against the headboard, and René stared out the window.

Before I could speak, Heather told Francine that her father wanted to talk something over with her. I was taken aback by Heather calling me Francine's father, but I realized that she was making the point that Francine still had a parent who would look after her, who cared for her. I tried to outline Francine's options as fairly and as gently as I could: stay in Canada and live with her aunt Caroline or with René, or come to the United States and live with me. Before I could go on, Francine asked, "What would you like, Papa?"

As I answered that I wanted her to live with me more than anything in the whole world, to be close to me, to make up for all the time we'd lost, I felt my throat tighten.

"There's your answer," Heather said.

Francine smiled and looked to René. "And what do you think, Grand-Uncle?"

René didn't speak but continued to stare out the window. Finally, he turned. He was crying. "You must go with your father. It is what your mother wanted. I know him and know he will be a good father and you will be very happy. I will miss you, but we will never lose touch. That is my solemn promise."

"And who will be my mother?" Francine said.

Heather gave me a sharp look and sat upright on the bed. "Maisie. Fran's...your father's...your father's wife in America."

Francine folded her hands in her lap and turned her thumbs as though she were preparing another question.

I told her that it was complicated, but that we'd have plenty of time to talk about it, although I wasn't at all that confident in what I found himself saying next. "You will love Maisie, and she'll be a wonderful mother and friend to you. You'll see."

"Promise, Papa?"

"I promise," I said, and I sat on the bed and pulled my daughter to me, hoping that I could live up to the most important promise of my life.

Midmorning, after Lisette's Service, Heather and I packed up all of Francine's earthly belongings and began the long drive back to

Philadelphia. When we arrived in Bryn Mawr, the front door was unlocked, and I thought that somehow the house didn't feel like it had been empty for two weeks. I took Francine by the hand and led her to the dining area that looked out on the terrace, where we found Maisie kneeling with her back to us, weeding her garden in the dwindling September daylight while Oscar Mayer slept curled in a ball next to her.

I was at a loss for words and blurted out, "Anybody home?"

Maisie turned and without hesitation, as though she knew all along how things would unfold, said, "Hi, Francine. I'm so very happy that you've come home." She smiled at me and said, "Hi, you," and reached to shake Francine's outstretched hand.

They studied each other for a brief moment without speaking until Francine broke the silence by saying, "I am happy to meet you, Mama," and the next thing I knew they were crying and clinging to one another with Oscar Mayer wagging his tail and pawing at their legs.

It was the happiest moment of my life, and I thought that all the pain had been worth it, that things had a very good chance of turning out okay after all.

Clearing the Air

Dad called me early the following day to tell me that Mom was in the Chestnut Hill hospital. Her liver was failing, and she had a lot of fluid in her abdomen. He said she had cirrhosis, and he'd like me to visit her that afternoon and, if at all possible, come back to Twelve-Twelve for supper.

When I entered Mom's room, she welcomed me in French, saying that it was so nice to see me again. I must have seemed puzzled by her greeting, because Dad quickly said, "Gay, it's our son, Fran."

She muttered, *"D'accord.* Our dear son, Francis," and asked if I'd brought my sister with me. I started to answer, but Dad interrupted again and said that Heather had already been there but had promised to come back in the morning.

Mom smiled vacantly and asked, "Are you both still living at Twelve-Twelve?"

Our conversation continued on this confused track, back and forth between my mother's French and my English, until she said that it was time for her nap and closed her eyes and almost instantly fell asleep.

Once back home, Dad offered me a beer and poured himself a glass of tonic and then said, "Ah, what the hell," and added a slug of gin. We walked out onto the terrace and continued across the small stretch of lawn. A breeze stirred the copper-colored leaves of the giant beeches that framed the pool, and I felt a familiar sense of comfort and an unanticipated sense of ease. For a moment we both looked around the pool as though we were inspecting its surroundings. Dad raised his glass to mine. There was great sadness in the look he gave me. "To Lisette and better times," he said. Then, as though the thought had surprised him, he said that it was the first drink he'd had in almost eight years.

I started to say something, but Dad shook his head and said no, he wasn't struggling with a problem, that I'd seen the problem that he'd been dealing with at the hospital. He slumped into one of the Salterini chairs at the edge of the pool and placed his drink—untouched—at his feet and leaned forward and ran his hands over what was left of his short-cropped gray hair. "I'm sorry," he said. "I screwed up with your mother. And I owe you an apology because I've screwed up with you too."

I stood behind him, set my beer by his chair, and found my hands reaching for him as though I had no control over them. I kneaded the taut muscles in his shoulders and told him that we still had time to work things out, that we had a lot to talk about.

Surprisingly—it may have been Dad's uncharacteristic openness, although I really don't know why—I found myself confessing that Maisie and I had briefly separated. "All this business about us not being able to have kids hit her really hard," I said. "Really, really hard, because she wants kids so badly. And, when she has a problem, she needs lots of space and takes her time to work things through. The good news is that she's done all that, and we're back together."

"I'm glad to hear that, but I'm not surprised," my father said. "I know it's been tough on you both." He paused. "I'm guessing you've got more to tell me."

"Right, there's plenty more, but let's start with these." I placed the dingy Saran Wrap packet and his St. Christopher's medal in his hand and asked him to read what I'd handed him. As he untaped the packet and opened the envelope it protected, I quieted my hands and leaned against the back of his chair and silently read the letter over his shoulder.

July 7, 1959
Dear Mom and Dad:

Hopefully this is a letter you'll never have to read, but I'm writing it in case something happens to me during my tour here. The odds of anything happening are small, for none of our advisers have been seriously injured to date, although there have been some close calls on patrols or with crazies throwing grenades at our headquarters. Nonetheless, tomorrow the company I'm assigned to goes on its first real attempt to make contact with the Viet Cong and, as you know, Dad, in this business anything can happen.

So, where to start?

First, to me, a twenty-two-year-old shavetail (does that make you smile, Dad?) who doesn't know squat about international politics, it's not real clear why we're here, why we're involved in someone else's civil war, even though we're told repeatedly that we're helping stop the spread of communism—the domino effect and the "yellow peril"— but none of us, including my CO, are all that sure.

I can assure you, however, that I do know at least a couple of reasons why I'm here, which I hope in some way will be helpful to you. I signed up for this tour because I was bored by the prospect of spending another year at Fort Bragg. Coming here had an aura of excitement, perhaps even glamour, and gave me the opportunity to see a country I barely knew existed. As I write this, I doubt that all that's worth dying for, but it's too late now. As a lot of us in country say, it is what it is.

And, as Dad knows, it's not always why you're fighting that becomes most important, but who's fighting at your side. So once again, if something should happen to me, I thought you should know who will be with me at the time. Like all of us here, the four guys who make up my team are all regular army volunteers who look after each other like brothers, and I feel a closeness to them that I've never felt before, even with friends like Potter. Right now they're like family to me. My medic is Maurice Henderson and happens to come from west Philadelphia near the Penn campus. He's only twenty and jokes around a lot but is bright as hell and hopes to go to nursing or medical school someday, and I hope he does. Ronald Nogowski (we all call him "Nogo") is from Brooklyn and is my radio operator. He's tough as nails and is getting married as soon as he gets back to the States. Both Nogo and Henderson are going with me tomorrow.

Ron Hutts is my demolition expert. He's from Joplin, Missouri, is very soft spoken, and may be the strongest man I've ever met—his biceps are bigger than my thighs and covered with tattoos! And our automatic-weapons expert, Pedro Diaz, is from San Juan. He spends his free time serenading us with his guitar, singing what sound like real sad ballads in Spanish. I don't know why I told you about these guys except that they're the people who trust their lives to me, and vice versa, and tonight that seems very important to me. They're my buddies even though I'm their leader.

But, back to why I'm here. To be honest with you, Mom and Dad, I thought another year at a greater distance from you would help me sort out my feelings about the things that took place between us before I went to Dartmouth and how you treated Lisette. I'm sure it won't come as a surprise to you that I think about that almost daily, reflecting on how I handled things and how you did in turn. In many ways I owe you an apology for being so hard headed, for not taking your advice more seriously, and for leaving Dartmouth so quickly. But—and this is a big BUT for me—while I can understand all the reasons you thought Lisette was the wrong girl for me—or was she just wrong for the Delafield family?—you never understood how much I loved her, and still do. So as you go on with your lives, remember that Lisette was your son's one true love and be thankful that we were together, even though it was only for a short period of time.

In so many other ways, you've been great parents, and Heather has not only been a terrific big sister but has always been one of my best friends. Please know that I'll always love you and Heather and have tried to be a son, and a brother, who you could be proud of, although I know I may have made that difficult at times. I hope you'll forgive me as I forgive you.

Well, time to go. I'll tape this inside my helmet with the hope that no one ever reads it but me. For you, Mom, I'll sign it, votre très dévoué et respectueux fils.

And, Dad, I'll take your St. Christopher's medal with me tomorrow, for luck and to remind me of you.

Please know that I love you both,
Fran
P.S. Say hi to Potter for me and tell him to behave.

Dad folded the letter and looked back at me over his shoulder. His eyes were filled with tears. "And to think I made it home without a scratch." He paused and smiled. "I'm glad I didn't have to read this in 1959."

"Me too." I settled in the chair next to him. "There's more."

"There's no time like the present," he said, the way he used to when Heather and I were kids. He started to hand the letter back to me but stopped. "Could I read this to your mother? It might make things easier for her."

I told him that I'd very much like Mom to see it, and Dad slipped the letter in his pants pocket, lit a cigarette, and nodded at me as though he was ready to listen.

I explained that much of what I was about to tell him was going to surprise him and that a lot of it wasn't going to please him. He said that he was a "big boy," big enough to handle the truth, and for a moment I wondered which of us was the parent and which the child.

I started at the very beginning of our troubles, with me not being able to tell Mom and him why Potter and I had left La Malbaie. Dad just nodded a few times and quietly smoked his cigarette. I had an urge to ask him what he was thinking but, instead, leaned forward in my chair to make it clear that I wanted his undivided attention. I told him the entire story of Lisette, the most important story in my life told in no more than a sentence for each thing I wanted my father to know and understand:

I loved Lisette very much.

She never finalized our divorce.

She had our child, a girl named Francine, and Maisie and I were going to raise her.

I paused to gain my composure because, once again, I felt my anger and resentment building but knew that Heather was right: this was about understanding and forgiving. Nonetheless, I wouldn't have been honest with my father, or myself, if I hadn't said, "So you see, you and Mom got Lisette wrong from the start."

Dad ground his cigarette out on the flagstone with his shoe and put his hands over his mouth and nose and shook his head. "I'm so sorry. She was such a lovely, honest girl. And so beautiful." Tears streamed down his cheeks. "Under the right circumstances…" He paused. "She would have made you very happy."

"Then why?" I said. "Why did you let Mom drive her away?"

"Guilt," Dad said. He stood and brushed his hands at his tears. He fumbled for another cigarette but left his hands in his pockets and took a deep breath. "Okay. This isn't going to please you, either. Heather knows it all because your mother confided the whole nasty thing to her in a drunken state." He drew another heavy breath. "At first it drove a wedge between Heather and me. Now, thankfully, we've talked it through and are back on an even keel. So please, Fran, try to understand. Please?" He paused again. "The years during the war and right after were extremely difficult for many of us. Like so many couples who had been separated for several years, after I came home, your mother and I had a hard time adjusting to our new life together. On top of that, the amount she drank surprised me because she was nothing more than a social drinker when the war began, but by the time the war was over, things had changed. On several occasions she became drunk and angry enough that I had to physically restrain her. In all fairness to her, I think your uncle Robert's suicide just after V-E Day contributed greatly to her problems. She worshipped her brother and frequently referred to him as *la crème de la crème*, and I don't think she ever really recovered from what he did. So many people were losing their loved ones to the war, it must have made it all the more difficult for her to lose her only brother to depression and drink, and then see me come home without a scratch.

"What's more, my practice was slow to pick up, and I was so traumatized by what I'd experienced in Belgium—there were tragedies like the one in Malmedy that never made the news—that there were times, sometimes even days on end, that I sat at my drafting table fidgeting and doing nothing. More than once I threatened to leave the firm; for what, I had no idea."

He nodded a number of times without speaking, as though he was gathering his thoughts. Or his courage. "Between the problems at the office and at home, I felt like I was caught between a rock and a hard place, that I needed a friend and…well…one thing led to another, and Anita and I had what your mother described as a 'fling,' although it was far more—and lasted far longer—than a fling. Your mother found out about our relationship shortly before you graduated from Episcopal, and it made for a very long, unhappy Memorial Day weekend. I'd registered Anita and me as Mr. and Mrs. Delafield at a motel in Kennett Square, where I was designing a new school, and naively used our home address. Shortly after that, the motel sent a note that your mother opened saying they hoped we'd enjoyed our stay. When she confronted me, she called Anita a social-climbing Irish Catholic who hoped to benefit from our fine Philadelphia name and said she was surprised that she hadn't already 'played the pregnancy card.' She also said that all I was interested in was Anita's 'full figure' and insisted that I fire her. Both Anita and I agreed it would be best if we cleared the slate and started anew, and she left the firm, unfortunately under a cloud of suspicion."

I raised a hand for him to pause for a moment. "But Anita never stopped sending her cards. She seemed to know so much about Heather and me."

"That's because she views Heather and you as part of her family and…" He looked down and sighed. "And we still see each other. Not a lot, but, try as we might, we can't cut it off, I guess because neither of us really wants to, although for a while Anita halfheartedly searched for a husband before she accepted that she couldn't marry someone else feeling the way she did about me.

"So that's the dilemma I faced when Lisette entered the picture. Your mother saw a similar pattern emerging between you and Lisette that Anita and I had experienced, even though it wasn't the same: I was having a relationship outside my marriage; you were marrying the girl you loved. Nonetheless, your mother shamed me into taking a hard line with you to prove that I'd learned my lesson.

In many ways I think it was her way of asking for my final apology, although she never gave me her final forgiveness."

Dad freed a cigarette from his pack and snapped his lighter open and closed. He was as animated as I had ever seen him, and I sat in silence waiting for him to finish. "I was paying my debt, Fran, trying to show your mother that I wouldn't let you get involved with someone who wasn't to the manor born. Who was a Catholic. Who might have been after our money, even though there wasn't any. I ended up punishing you for my mistakes, and I'm sorry, truly sorry. And I'm sorry for my insinuations about Lisette's character. I still shudder when I think that I called her a tramp. She was anything but, and I now know she may be the most courageous, honorable girl I've ever met."

He paused and asked if I was ready for the last insult.

I shrugged and said, "Why not?"

"Okay," he said. "When you started dating a girl with Maisie's reputation, all our past issues boiled to the surface once again. I'd be less than honest if I didn't tell you that at first—but only at first—I wished you'd chosen a girl with a different image, mainly because of the bind her reputation put me in with your mother. But that's changed. I've grown to love Maisie and her sense of humor, and I enjoy how much you seem to love her, especially after the heartbreak with Lisette. And your mother talks about you and Lisette shaming the Delafield name? In many ways I'm so ashamed of what I did, and I'm worried sick about how you'll view me now that I've told you."

He shook his head to signal that he wasn't through. "But in my defense, if you'll permit that, I was confused about whom to be loyal to, the ones I loved or the woman I'd committed to. I know this ambivalence made my behavior seem, if not weak, difficult to understand. But there were sound arguments for you not to get married at the time that had nothing to do with Lisette's background or religion. You both were so young. You hadn't even started college, didn't have a job, and her inability to speak English isolated—"

"You never gave her a chance to learn," I interrupted.

"I know, and I'm sorry," he said. "And ashamed. Like the other mistakes, now there's nothing that can be done."

I wanted to tell him right then and there about Francine but thought it was more important to hear him out. "What else?"

He continued to fidget with his lighter. "Your mother's going to die because of me. As miserable as she made me, she was my wife, my responsibility, and I chose to be an enabler. Look where it got me. Just because she never was really outrageous—you know, a falling-down drunk—I chose the path of least resistance. While you were in the army and Heather was living with us after Vassar, she tried to convince me to get your mother some help, even suggested I threaten a divorce. I resisted for so long—and so hard—that your sister finally gave up."

I said I understood.

"I hope so, but I wouldn't blame you if you don't," Dad said. "Getting your mother help would have been the right thing to do, but goddamn it, son, it's so easy to talk about yet so hard to do. Who knows? It might have been even more uncomfortable than living with her as a relatively happy drunk."

He finally lit the cigarette he was holding. For a moment he lazily moved it in a figure eight and then said he had a question for me. "How do you feel about me cheating on your mother? That's what I did, you know, cheated on her."

Again I said that I understood, not only what he'd done but why. I added that up until recently, I wouldn't have had the capacity to understand.

"Or to forgive?"

"Now I think I can do both," I said, and in my mind I could hear Reverend Crawford saying that occasionally you've got to give people an intentional pass to win the game. While I admit that when I was at Episcopal I never really understood what he was trying to tell me, at that moment I did, and I thought that's just the way things are, even in the best of families.

"Thank God," Dad said and smoked his cigarette in silence. When he was finished, he put his hand on my arm. "I feel like a huge weight has been lifted from my shoulders. Now, tell me all about your daughter...my granddaughter Francine." He smiled. "Tell me all."

"Un Début"

The next morning, well before it was time for me to wake Maisie and Francine, I was picking at my cereal and skimming the *Inquirer*, trying to find something that would hold my attention, when the phone rang. It was Dad. He began by saying that, after I'd left Twelve-Twelve he'd gone back to the hospital and read my letter to my mom, and she seemed to appreciate it.

"Seemed to?"

Dad's voice broke when he said, "She wasn't really aware of me being there, but I read it to her anyway. It meant so much to me, and I pray to her." He paused and cleared his throat. "Fran, your mother died at quarter to six this morning. The last words she uttered were '*un début.*' Perhaps she was looking forward to what came next, or it was an apology of sorts. Maybe it was her way of giving us permission to start anew."

As Dad told me this, I was overcome with regret about the unforgiving manner in which I'd related to Mom when what she needed most was my help and my love, even though I thought that, at some level, she was aware of the damage she was doing but didn't have the ability, or the will, to stop. But now she was gone, without me having a chance to explain things to her, to apologize for my behavior, and to say a proper good-bye.

I woke Maisie to give her the news. She said she was worried that on top of Lisette's death, all of this was becoming too much for me, and she began to cry. When I said not to worry, that I was okay, that I'd been steeling myself for this for a number of days, Maisie smiled through her tears and said that, as always, I was putting up a good front but that she didn't believe a word I said. She reached for my hand and insisted that she tell Francine, that it would be their first real mother-daughter talk, and she'd like that very much.

Before driving to Chestnut Hill, I called Potter at Episcopal, where he'd recently begun teaching history and coaching squash and tennis. I told him about Mom and said I was kind of in a daze, that I had mixed feelings that I wasn't too proud of, and that the whole thing was complicated as hell.

"I'll bet," Potter said, "but you're not to blame. You tried to be a good son, Delafield. You really did. I know it's not easy to hear right now, but your mom never gave you much of a chance." He asked that I tell Dad how sorry he was and that he'd see him, and all of us, at the funeral. He chuckled. "To cheer you a bit, Delafield, this generation of kids is no different than when we were here. The little weenies still try to hide their hard-ons in their blue serge suits when they march out of chapel, and they ogle Deirdre just the way we used to pant after some of the hotter faculty wives. It's good for Deirdre's ego and makes me laugh my ass off. A lot of stuff never seems to change."

When we hung up, I thought that, as imperfect a friend as Potter had been at times, he was the closest thing to a brother I'd ever have, and his comments comforted me. These thoughts caused me to smile and tear at the same time as I hurried to Twelve-Twelve to check in on Dad.

Mom's funeral was held at St. Paul's Church on the last Saturday in September. Although Dad never got a chance to talk with her about her service, he'd sketched it out as he thought she would have wanted it. He told Heather and me that he didn't want any remembrances—he thought they might be a little awkward, perhaps even painful—but asked each of us to read a lesson, Heather from the Old Testament and me from the New.

While I don't remember many of the details of the service, there were a few I'll never forget. First, Heather was vintage Heather. She read her lesson from Ecclesiastes with such presence and authority that it almost took my breath away. But at the lesson's close, "a time to love, and a time to hate; a time for war, and a time for peace," she looked out over the congregation with a gentle smile and recited her own version: "a time to love, and a time for peace." When she slipped by me to take her seat, she whispered, "A time for hate and a time for war? They couldn't have been serious."

Second, I couldn't help but wonder if Dad's asking me to read the lesson from Corinthians—"When I was a child, I spoke like a child, I thought like a child, I reasoned like a child; when I became an adult, I put an end to childish ways"—was a gentle nudge from him to have me take a closer look at how I'd handled things after I'd returned from La Malbaie, and how I'd behave differently in the future.

But what I remember the most was the order in which Dad directed the family to file into our pew: he would lead, followed by Francine; next Maisie and me; then Heather with her daughter, Louisa; and finally, Trey. It wasn't the order in which we entered the pew that was so important, it was the order in which it caused us to leave the service, with all of Dad's friends, and Maisie's and mine, to see.

Once the minister had finished the benediction and the familiar strains of "Onward Christian Soldiers" filled the church, Dad took Francine's hand and led her down the aisle with a tight-lipped smile, nodding to a number of his friends, occasionally reaching for their hands. For an instant I imagined the silver lieutenant colonel's oak leaf on his collar and saw the man who once had been my hero—the man who had lived in his wife's boozy shadow for so many years—finally taking a stand, seeming to signal, "This is my granddaughter, and I'm damn proud of her." And I never felt so proud to be his son as I did at that moment.

Maisie took my arm, and we followed Dad and Francine. As we approached the last pew, out of the corner of my eye I saw Anita sitting alone, dabbing a handkerchief at her tears, staring straight ahead, clearly not wanting to make eye contact with anyone or be noticed. I stopped for a second, leaned toward her, and said that Dad would need her now more than ever. She thanked me and said that he would need his family most of all and blew a kiss to Maisie as though she'd known her all her life.

Outside the church I said to Maisie, "That wasn't so painful. Or was it?"

"It was beautiful. Perfect." She pulled me to her, kissed me on the cheek, and kept her mouth close to my ear. "Thanks for sticking by me," she whispered. "I'll make this new deal work. Just you wait and see."

Dad, Heather, and I were pleased to see so many people at the service and afterward in the church's parish hall where we accepted an outpouring of kind and understanding comments about Mom and our loss.

As you might expect, Maisie and I got lots of questions about Francine. Had we adopted her? We answered yes, we were beginning the process, that her mother was a close Canadian friend who had died unexpectedly. How did her father feel? We said that he'd abandoned her mother before she was born but was delighted that she was in such loving hands.

Neat, tight, and pretty much the truth.

Once the formalities were over and the well-wishers had formed into small groups, Dad, Heather, and Trey joined Maisie, Francine, and me for a family huddle. "A toast," Heather said, raising her glass of iced tea. "To Mom. Far from perfect, but always trying to do what she thought was right."

As we raised our glasses, I added, "*Un début*," and Heather and Dad repeated it in unison.

Maisie gave me a quizzical look. "*Un début?* What's that all about?"

I told her they were Mom's last words, that they may have been her way of giving us permission to start over, maybe even her way of asking for our forgiveness.

"Wow," Maisie said. "Really?"

For the first time since Mom had died, my father welled up. "Really," he choked out. "So let's not disappoint her. Let's do it right."

Maisie nodded and, to my surprise and delight, raised her glass. "To Mom Delafield, and to my adorable new daughter. And to all of us."

As we reached to touch one another, mingling our hands and arms, kisses and tears, I thought, yes, to all of us. A family once again.

Acknowledgments

I'm indebted to novelist Ellen Lesser, whose editorial insights amazed and energized me; and to Peter Moister, whose heartfelt discussions about fighting in Vietnam were informative and entertaining, brightening several humdrum writing days.

Also, many thanks to Chris Noel for his early reading of this story; to retired Marine Corps captain Jim Talone for his graphic and chilling descriptions of firefights in Vietnam; to Dr. Kaighn Smith, who patiently answered all my many questions about infertility; and to Dr. Chat Lee for painting a broad picture of how alcoholism was handled by many families during the years in which the fictional Delafields struggled with the problem.

Additional thanks to Major Crystal Boring, chief of public affairs, and Donna Tabor, command historian, both assigned to the XVIII Airborne Corps and Fort Bragg, and my great friend Mike Overlock. Their informative and timely answers to my endless questions were most helpful.

(photo by Deirdre Snyder)

About the Author

Harry Groome is the author of the novels *Wing Walking* and *Thirty Below* and the award-winning Stieg Larsson parody *The Girl Who Fished with a Worm*. Harry has been a finalist for the William Faulkner Short Story Awards and has been nominated for the Pushcart Prize. His short stories, poems, and articles have appeared in dozens of magazines and anthologies, including *Gray's Sporting Journal*, *Ellery Queen's Mystery Magazine*, *Descant*, and *Detroit Magazine*, and two of his stories have been performed by the InterAct Theatre Company in Philadelphia as part of its *Writing Aloud* series. Harry is a graduate of the University of Pennsylvania and holds an MFA in Writing from the Vermont College of Fine Arts. He and his wife, Lyn, divide their time between Villanova, Pennsylvania, and the Adirondack Mountains in New York. Visit Harry at www.harrygroome.com.